The path led directly up to the low porch of the golf clubhouse. They turned then to start back. Karen was suddenly anxious again to make plans for getting home, any way she could.

Neither one of them noticed the man who was standing inside the clubhouse, watching. He was the grounds keeper for the club. An unimportant man, even to the organization he did an occasional job for. But he'd been alerted along with many others. The organization was very thorough, computerized, in fact. He had a hunch this was the girl they wanted back. They'd mentioned a boy too. And this was just the sort of deserted, off-season place they might run to.

Perfect for them, except there is no perfect hiding place, especially on an island. He couldn't be sure, of course, until he'd had a look round for the car. But he always played his hunches.

RICHARD PECK was born in Decatur, Illinois. He attended Oxford University in England and holds degrees from DePauw University and Southern Illinois University. He is the author of *Secrets of the Shopping Mall*, *Are You in the House Alone?*, *Ghosts I Have Been*, *Representing Super Doll*, *Dreamland Lake*, and *Close Enough to Touch* (all available in Dell Laurel-Leaf editions). His adult novel, *New York Time*, was recently published by Delacorte Press. Mr. Peck lives in New York City.

THROUGH A BRIEF DARKNESS

Richard Peck

LAUREL-LEAF BOOKS

LAUREL-LEAF BOOKS bring together under a single imprint outstanding works of fiction and nonfiction particularly suited for young adult readers, both in and out of the classroom. Charles F. Reasoner, Professor Emeritus of Children's Literature and Reading, New York University, is consultant to this series.

Published by
Dell Publishing Co., Inc.
1 Dag Hammarskjold Plaza
New York, New York 10017

Laurel-Leaf Library ® TM 766734,
Dell Publishing Co., Inc.

ISBN: 0-440-98809-8

RL: 5.2

Reprinted by arrangement with The Viking Press
Printed in the United States of America
First Laurel-Leaf printing—September 1982

*For Mair and Anthony Elliot of
Castle Rock in Devon*

THROUGH
A BRIEF
DARKNESS

1

The week before Karen was taken out of public school, she found the verse scrawled in grease pencil on the mirror of the six-grade girls' washroom:

> Andreas daddys a fireman
> Carmens fathers a cook
> Rachels dad is a doctor
> But Karens old man is a CROOK

It wasn't the kind of thing she could tell the family housekeeper they had then. She had to save it up until her father came home from a business trip. Because she was twelve that year, it never occurred to her not to tell it at all. And because she was twelve, she wanted everything that happened to have a happy ending. So when she told him, she tried to laugh around a lump in her throat. Then she waited for Dad to laugh with her, to laugh it all away.

Instead, his face went dark, and he said, "I won't have my little girl coarsened by a trashy public school atmosphere." And that's all he said.

The next week she was enrolled in a private day school across town—Birchampton School—where she spent the rest of the sixth grade a stranger.

But she didn't go back there for seventh grade. She was prepared to. She'd come home from camp on a sunny August day to go shopping with Miss Simon,

her father's secretary. The stores were full of Back to
School clothes in window settings of little red school-
houses and yellow maple leaves. Miss Simon flashed
Dad's credit card all over town. They had lunch at the
counter in Bloomingdale's surrounded by packages.
And when Karen came home to the big rambling
apartment on East End Avenue, she found the letter.

It was on the floor in Dad's study. She hadn't meant
to read it. But it was on school stationery, signed by
the headmistress herself. And it was there on the rug
where he had dropped it.

THE BIRCHAMPTON SCHOOL
Founded in 1894
"Here We Educate for a Fuller Life"

Dear Mr. Beatty:
    It is with a profound sense of regret that I am
called upon to inform you that we cannot accept
your daughter, Karen, as a student again for this
autumn term . . .

What have I done? Karen wondered. What have I
done?

    This is a matter of some delicacy, and not, I
assure you, a decision entered upon lightly. I am,
after all, responsible to the Birchampton Board of
Governors, the Birchampton Parents Organization, to my staff, to our students, and above all,
to the proud traditions of The Birchampton
School.
    We pride ourselves at Birchampton in the prac-
tice of democratic standards and a sense of fair
play. To pry into the family backgrounds of our
students is personally repugnant to me.

Nonetheless, it has been brought to my attention repeatedly by a number of our parents who insist upon anonymity that given distasteful allegations leveled against her father in the press and the innuendoes of persistent rumor, Karen is no longer a suitable classmate for Birchampton students . . .

Karen struggled to follow the long sentences, the twisted loops of words. It's not because of me, she thought. It's something about Daddy.

I am in no position to pass personal judgment on intimations of illegal connections any parent of a student has or is said to have . . .

She sweated over this letter, Karen thought.

but I must ask you to consider the heavy responsibility I bear to our students and to their parents. It is not necessary, I am sure, to remind you that Birchampton's high academic *and social* standards are maintained by a commensurately high tuition fee and the most meticulous process of student selection. Our parents, therefore, have a right in determining their children's associates. The continuance of our traditions depends upon their financial and moral support.

I have, believe me, anguished over this decision. Moreover, I have taken into consideration the fact that Karen's mother is no longer living and the particular difficulties of rearing a daughter in a motherless home.

I can only hope you will understand my position in this painful matter and will make other arrangements for Karen's education. Please find enclosed the check forwarded to our bursar by

your secretary for the semester tuition which I am
returning to you . . .

Karen looked down at the rug. It was littered with
small yellow scraps of a torn-up check.

YOURS VERY SINCERELY,
Minerva Hudson, Ph.D.

To hell with them. Karen thought, and her eyes
filled with tears. To hell with Ph.D. Hudson and the
proud, snotty Birchampton tradition.

Then she walked back to the front hall where the
boxes of her new school clothes were still in the
Bloomingdale's shopping bag. She jammed her coin
purse down into its depths. Then she walked out of
the apartment, dragging the paper bag into the eleva-
tor and through the marble lobby. If she had a plan, it
was to get downtown to Grand Central Station and
take the first train somewhere. *There's no place for
me,* she told herself on the subway. *I won't even be
missed.*

She sat in the waiting room at Grand Central until
after dark. She sat there through the rush hour while
galloping commuters tried to trample the droopy
shopping bag. A skinny, leggy little figure in a river
of people who all had someplace to go. But since she
didn't and since there was no Miss Simon to buy her a
ticket, she came home finally to the big shadowy
apartment. And since it was the housekeeper's day
off, there was no one there to wonder where she'd
been.

Something about being twelve kept Karen from asking herself the questions that no one else was there to
answer. Just being twelve—and alone—was hard
enough to face.

* * *

At the last minute, Miss Simon with her computerized efficiency got Karen into a boarding school. Not a *great* boarding school, but one a long way from New York. Somehow Karen knew they were trying to protect her, trying to get her away from "the innuendoes of persistent rumor," whatever that meant.

Her father wrote her regularly, though the words on the pages were flawlessly typed by Miss Simon on the office IBM electric. In October he wrote to tell her he'd let the housekeeper go. "We won't need her anymore, kitten. From now on it'll be just the two of us together on your school holidays. We won't need anybody else."

But in the years after, it was rarely the two of them together. That first Christmas, her father was out of the country—either Puerto Rico or Portugal. Karen wasn't sure. Her geography was shaky. She was still trying to live in a child's small world.

Finally, her father gave up the big apartment on East End Avenue and moved into a studio only big enough for himself. There was just no need for a home anymore.

Miss Simon took full command of the necessary arrangements. After a while, she became the only roots Karen had. As far as she knew, Miss Simon never left New York. She was always there in the trim little suit and horn rims. Karen always found her waiting under the clock at Grand Central or standing by the gate at La Guardia with a flat folder of tickets, travelers checks, and a neatly typed address to the next destination. She shunted Karen from school to camp, from camp to school, from school to school—like a sleek, nearly human switch engine.

Miss Simon continued to do the shopping, with carte blanche from Dad. There was less and less time for Karen to shop with her in New York. For summer camp a bag full of "active sportswear" from Abercrombie & Fitch with the name tags sewn in by the alterations department. In the fall, Miss Simon was at her post again with a fresh supply of school clothes—well chosen and safe. Semihippie shifts for that first school up in Vermont which was mildly experimental and very heavy on pottery making. And for the eighth grade, since Dad wanted her to change schools, riding clothes for the Dominion School in Virginia where being horsey meant a weekly trip up to the stable.

It was at the Dominion School that she met Bea Callaghan from New Jersey. Bea was a big girl with an even bigger voice, and there was something about her that made the rest of the girls keep their distance. She was a little gross, they all said. Which meant that she didn't blend in as smoothly as Karen had learned to do. And another thing about Bea: the social refinements were lost on her. Practically every time she got on a horse, she fell off.

They'd never talked. But one day Karen was out riding when Bea came cantering up on a nag that sagged noticeably under her undistributed weight.

"You're a damn long way from the ground on one of these things, aren't you?" Bea gasped out, trying to hitch up her Levis without leaving the saddle.

They rode along a fence row together and across a field that was part pasture, part campus. Karen could sense Bea's need for someone to talk to—someone who wouldn't brand her gross.

"Well, I guess they found the right place for us," she said at last, trying to coax her horse nearer Karen's.

"What do you mean, Bea?"

"Oh come on. You know."

Karen didn't. But she knew she was about to.

"I mean we're okay here. They're not going to throw us out. They're too desperate for the tuition money.

Don't let anybody kid you about the big prestige of Dominion. They're lucky if they can pay the water bill."

"Why would they try to throw us out anyway?" Karen asked. Silence would have seemed like a turn-off to Bea. And besides, the Birchampton School was a world away from these Virginia mountains.

"Because of all that dirty money our fathers make that keeps us here. Some of the little princesses around here haven't got—"

"I don't know what you're talking about," Karen said and felt that something inevitable was catching up with her. She dug her heel in the horse's side. But it did no good. None of the horses really moved unless they were pointed towards the stable.

"Maybe you don't," Bea said. "Maybe you really don't. You can kid yourself all you want to, stuck away down here. Like these southern belles who swear they just came off the old plantation."

"What does it matter where you came from?"

"It shouldn't. But it does to you and me. The year I was in third grade my Dad was doing time—he was in jail, to spell it out. Income tax evasion was the charge. But they were out to get him for anything they could. He's a key man in the Jersey territory. He came out of jail richer than he went in."

Karen was silent then, not caring what Bea thought and dazed by the boasting in her voice.

"Your Dad could be doing time right now."

"You don't know any—"

"But I know he isn't."

"How do you know anything about him?"

"Well, for one thing," Bea said, "I'm the only inmate of this so-called school who reads the New York papers in the library. Don't sweat it. Even the librarian doesn't read them."

Karen was trying to withdraw, not wanting to hear

what this big, loud—this gross—girl was saying. Yet
she knew if Bea galloped off into the sunset, she'd
follow her. And make her tell everything she knew.

"And your Dad's very big in the New York operation. In fact he practically *is* the New York operation."

"What operation?"

"Numbers. Shakedowns. Protection. Influence ped-
dling. Phony real-estate deals. The whole bit. Look,
I'm not blaming you for not knowing—and I can see
you don't. Your Dad's smooth. Mine isn't. My old
man's kind of a hangover from the past. Yours can
work both sides of the street and still come out like
Mister Clean."

"Shut up," Karen said, but too quietly. Louder, she
said, "Newspapers don't—"

"I know. Newspapers don't tell you everything. But
I got my education from bodyguards. Yeah, I had one
to take me to school and pick me up every day before
I came here. Those guys'll tell you what nobody else
will. They're smarter than they look. You know I
really miss them down here in this hole."

"And your folks sent you here because they thought
you didn't know."

"Are you kidding? My folks sent me down here to
protect my life."

That night Karen wrote to her father during study
hour:

> Dear Daddy,
>   I need to see you and to talk to you right away.
> It's urgent . . .

A letter came back, but it was from Miss Simon:

> Dear Karen,
>   Your father is away just now—in Las Vegas on

a much needed vacation. I hesitate to disturb him. Is there anything I can do for you?

But there wasn't.

It was a long time before Karen saw her father. So long that she changed. So long that she couldn't imagine what she'd have said to him if he'd come running to answer that first cry for help.

She learned how to handle herself, to protect herself, though she didn't quite know who she was. She could even handle Bea when the need arose. It mostly involved silence, and that began to lead to independence. Sometimes when the loneliness was too much, she'd write a letter. Not a letter to Dad that would be expertly slit open by Miss Simon first.

Instead, she'd write to Jay Fielding. It didn't matter that she hadn't seen Jay since the Wisconsin summer she was nine. It didn't even matter that she didn't know his address. Because she never mailed the letters.

Dear Jay,

Someday Daddy and I will be all alone. And he'll tell me everything the newspapers say and the rumors say and Bea says are hateful damn dirty lies . . .

Dear Jay,

When I see Dad again, I'm going to make him tell me the truth. He must think I'm an idiot he can send away to school like it was a mental hospital or something . . .

Dear Jay,

I'll tell him I know all about his big operations. And then I'm going to say, I cannot allow you to

support me with tainted money. I cannot be your
daughter anymore . . .

Dear Jay,
  It doesn't matter what he does, he's my father,
and I love him . . .

The day came, finally. It was in the spring after
Karen turned fourteen. On the way from the Dominion School to camp near Bar Harbor, she stopped over
in New York. For once, Dad replaced Miss Simon and
took her to the Plaza for lunch.

All those unmailed letters to Jay were a jumble in
her head, the letters and Bea and the far-off Birchampton School. She was afraid of being with him.
They were strangers.

But he was as shy as she was, acting like a young
boy on a first date. He reminded her of someone, a
type, really. Not a movie star exactly. Someone that
glamorous, but more responsible looking, dignified.
He kept twisting his wedding ring and fidgeting with
the flatware. She liked him for wearing the ring still.

Her mother wasn't even a memory to her. Perhaps
just the scent of lavender one night when Karen was
still in her bed with the sides. Her mother—someone—
bending to kiss her goodnight, some lavender-scented
presence, distant now. Her mother had been English.
Dad married her in London after the war, and she'd
died when Karen was three.

She struggled to think of something to break the
ice. "Do I look different, Daddy?" She sat up very
straight in the chair to give him a good view.

"You look wonderful, sweetheart. But you're growing up."

"And out," Karen said. "I'm developing a figure,
sort of." And he looked embarrassed, even shocked.
"Didn't you expect me to?"

"Well, yes, of course. But, you know, not so soon. I mean, I still think of you as a little girl. You'll always be—"

"Little like I was when we were together?"

"Yes, kitten, like that. Now let me have a look at the menu. Don't forget you have a plane to catch."

But she couldn't let him off that easily. Not after all this time. Not with the questions waiting in her mind. But what could she say to make him see she was old enough to know?

"What do you do, Daddy, for a living, I mean."

"I dabble," he said, not putting down his menu.

"What does that mean?"

"It means I put money in here and take it out there."

"Oh, Daddy, be more specific. I'm not a child."

"You keep reminding me of that."

Karen stared at her plate, waiting him out.

"Right now I have some money in a discotheque. That's a kind of night club."

"Oh, Daddy, I know what a discotheque is."

"Do they take you on night club field trips at the Dominion School?" He was slipping away. She could feel it. Something in her wanted him to. But she tried once more.

"What else do you do?"

"I work my fingers to the bone to educate my daughter because someday I'm going to be very proud of her."

"Aren't you proud of me right now?" she asked.

"Yes, sweetheart, prouder than I can tell you. You're . . . you're going to be a lot like your mother."

"In looks?"

"Yes. And maybe more than that." His hand with the wedding ring was resting on the table. Karen wanted to reach out and touch him, put her hand over his. But she didn't. It seemed too great a risk. He might draw away. For a moment, though, it was as if her mother was there. Not between them, but with them. A scent of lavender materializing into something more real, someone.

Maybe one day, Karen thought, I'll know what she was like, if I'm like her.

The thought of Bea crossed her mind again. Of what Bea and her father must talk about if they talked. But she erased them from her mind.

"Daddy, do you remember Minerva Hudson?"

"Who?"

"Minerva Hudson, Ph.D., the headmistress at Birchampton."

"No, honey. I don't believe I do."

2

By the time she was sixteen, Karen was a veteran of a whole catalogue of schools and camps. At least it seemed so to her. She'd graduated to counselor status at camp. She was the counselor that every new, homesick, scared kid rushed to for solace.

They fought to be assigned to her bunk or cabin or tent. She was always the big sister they wished they could adopt. It never occurred to any of them that the feeling might be mutual. She listened better than any adult to their tearful tales of pets left at home. And she seemed to know instinctively from the first-night campfire the young newcomer who would need her most.

At school she slipped inevitably into responsible positions, already knowing the ropes without having to be shown them.

The winter she was sixteen, Karen spent her junior year at the Isobel Kelvin Academy in Connecticut. It was a "farm atmosphere" school with painting classes in a silo and modern dance in the barn. From the windows of first period English class Karen could look out over the frozen hills, crisscrossed by brown hedges. Like an Andrew Wyeth landscape. She sat staring out of these windows on a March Monday while the teacher, Miss Sands, droned on about the Hobbits and man's need for fantasy.

Karen barely noticed when the door opened and the

office secretary everyone called "Bellringer" waddled in. On tiptoes she whispered something into Miss Sand's ear.

"Karen Beatty! To the office if you please!" Miss Sands called out. She had to say it twice in her loud, cultivated tone to bring Karen's mind in from the Wyeth fields.

Karen followed Bellringer down to the offices of the Headmistress. She was Miss Hervey, the great-niece of the original Isobel Kelvin. And she looked the part. As Karen went into the inner office, she could see that Miss Hervey was clearly overstimulated. "I have just had a call from your father's office in New York, Karen, and I hardly know what to make of it. Sit down, dear. Tell me, do you have your passport here at school?"

On the train to New York Karen leafed through the pages of her never used passport. The gray-green, mottled cover with the gold seal and her own personal serial number punched through in neat holes.

Inside, on the watery-blue pages her name, her birth-place, her height (five feet six inches), her hair (brown), her eyes (blue). Her picture, two years younger and gawky. Then the blank pages, waiting to be stamped in all those exotic places she'd hoped her father would take her. The rubber stamps that weren't there that might have said *Buenos Aires, Aruba, Tahiti, Portofino.*

Dad had always said it was a good idea to have an up-to-date passport because you never knew when you might be able to slip away for a few relaxing days in a new atmosphere. Karen had never quite given up hope that he'd take her with him one day.

Was this the day? She checked her watch as the train clattered through Old Greenwich. It was just the hour she should be in bio lab, squinting through a microscope at one-celled creatures with the other juniors. Instead, she was packed for a trip, long days before the legal Easter holiday, with her passport in hand. Her empty, promising passport.

It was a schoolgirl's dream, she thought. *Her* dream. To be sprung suddenly from school on the dullest Monday of the semester and spirited away to unknown adventure, and, hopefully, with Dad.

The train rumbled into the tunnel under Park Avenue. Suburban matrons coming to town to meet their husbands for dinner and a show clicked open their purses for a last-minute make-up check. It should have seemed to Karen like coming home, but it had been a long time since she'd called New York—or anyplace—home.

At Grand Central, Karen dragged her biggest suitcase and a canvas carryall into the main concourse. She barely glanced at the gigantic Kodak ad high on the wall, the grotesquely big full-color photo of two grinning lovers in a field of blinding springtime tulips. She headed straight for the clock in the middle of the floor that was always the rendezvous. She hoped it would be Dad standing there, but she was prepared to see the glint of Miss Simon's horn rims.

The clock meeting place was circled with strangers. Karen slowed down as she approached it, scanning the faces. A girl not much older than she stepped out of the crowd and headed for her.

"Hello, Karen," she said, a little breathless.

"I thought Dad or Miss Simon—"

"Oh, I know," the girl said, "but everything's in a mess at the office. Simon—I mean Miss Simon—is practically psyched out with everything she's supposed to do all at once. Mr. Beatty—your father, I mean—calls her every half hour from Miami. Or is it

Tampa? I forget. Anyway, he keeps calling and giving her more instructions. And you know how she is. *Super*-organized, but she's getting ready to snap. I was afraid I wouldn't know you. I've only seen you in that picture on your father's desk."

"But what's happening? And why—"

"Look," the girl said, "let me explain in the cab. Frankly, we're pushed for time. Simon has everything on a minute-by-minute schedule. And if I start balling things up, she'll have my head. I've only been in the office a couple of weeks. My name's Judy by the way. Here, let me help you with those bags."

There was a long yellow caravan of cabs edging down Lexington Avenue. Even with Karen's suitcase in tow, Judy nipped ahead of two businessmen waving for a taxi from the curb. Somehow, she managed to stop a cab that hadn't meant to, deliver instructions to the driver, and open the back door, pretty much all at once.

They were settled back in the seat and across the Forty-second Steet intersection before Karen could say, "But we're going downtown. Dad's office is the other—"

"Oh, but we're going right to the airport—J.F.K. Didn't they tell you at school? I heard Miss Simon say—Good grief! Does that mean you didn't bring your passport?"

"No, I've got it," Karen said, more bewildered than ever.

"Oh well, that's a relief anyway," Judy said and flopped back into the seat just as the cab dipped into the Midtown Tunnel. "It would have taken an act of Congress, *literally*, to get you out of the country without a passport."

"Out of the country?" Karen asked in a faint voice.

"Yes," Judy dug into a big, shoulder-strap bag,

"You're to be on the BOAC flight to London tonight, or I'm out of work. Here, wait a minute. This is going to explain things better than I can. You know Miss Simon. Put everything in writing is her *creed*."

From out of the depths of her handbag, Judy handed over a flat bundle that bore the familiar mark of Miss Simon efficiency. Karen sorted through it. In the fading light she was barely able to read the neat labels from Miss Simon's typewriter as the cab clipped along the highway through Queens.

> A plastic packet of British money ($250 worth) and a handy pocket conversion guide.
> A note indicating that an overseas checking account would be opened at a London bank in Karen's name.
> Identification labels for luggage.
> A one-way ticket on BOAC flight #909 to Heathrow Airport, London.

At the bottom of the bundle was a typed note from Miss Simon. It was obviously done in great haste because some of it tended to drift into shorthand and the signature was missing.

MEMO FROM JEANETTE TO *Karen*

> Because of some business problems that have suddenly arisen, yr father has to leave the country tonight. He will contact you as soon as possible in London.
> In the meantime, you are to stay in England with cousins of yr mother, Mr. & Mrs. Sydney Sutton. They will meet yr plane. But in the event of a foul-up their address is 73A Cornwall Gardens, London, S.W. 7.

It was almost evening when the cab edged over for the Van Wyck Expressway cutoff. The roadway was dark and slick beneath a blur of lights. A steady sleet was changing to snow. Sludge began to build up in wedges under the windshield wipers. The driver on the other side of the bulletproof divider swore to himself and strained over the statues on the dashboard. A big plane came in low over their heads, aiming for JFK.

"What business problem?" Karen said to Judy.

"I don't know. I'm new in the office, and it's all still a big blur."

"Tell me if you know," Karen said. "I'm not as innocent as I look." Judy was quiet for a moment. Finally she said, "I think it has something to do with the government or taxes or something like that. Honestly, I don't know. They don't tell me anything. But look, don't worry about it. I mean, these things happen, don't they?"

Judy sounded almost as if she wanted to be reassured. But all Karen could say was, "Nothing like this has ever happened before."

She couldn't really be sure of that much. All she knew was that she'd never been involved before. Maybe she'd been too young. Maybe she'd been kept safely tucked away in one school after another till now.

"It just seems so weird," Karen said. "If Miss Simon—"

"Look," Judy said, "maybe you can find out some more of the details from her. When you get to the airport, call her at the office. She'll probably be there till all hours."

The cab was making the big swing past the airline terminals; the road was jammed with traffic and glittering with lights through the snow. Beyond, the monster tails of the big 747's stood high above the buildings.

"Anyway," Judy was saying, "it'll be nice for you to see your cousins."

"I hope so," Karen said. "I didn't even know I had any."

The cab pulled into the line of cars unloading under the canopy of the BOAC-Air Canada building. "Well, this is it," Judy said. "Miss Simon told me to see you off, but do you think you can manage on your own? I mean you'll be boarding in a few minutes, and frankly I'm dying to get home, and I can keep this cab. I mean can you handle it?"

"Oh sure," Karen said. "This isn't my first flight, it's just the first one to—"

"London, Lady?" It was the baggage handler who had opened the cab door and was pulling Karen's suitcase out.

"Well, bon voyage and like that," Judy said. "Wish I was going with you." Then the cab was pulling away, and Karen followed her luggage into check-in, a little like a sleepwalker.

The big suitcase glided away from her and down a belt that disappeared into the floor. The agent stapled the baggage checks to her ticket and glanced at her passport. There was only a little time left.

Karen looked around the vast terminal room. Somber businessmen were having drinks in the English-styled pub. It was early evening yet, but some of the travelers were stretched out across the waiting-room seats, trying to doze. At the far end of the room there was a line of phone booths. Karen started toward them.

She let the phone ring twelve times, and then she dialed again. She could imagine the scene at the other end—vividly. The phone jangling in the empty office. Miss Simon gone for the night. Perhaps gone for good. The files standing open and her own picture on Dad's desk cleared away. As if none of them had ever existed. What could it mean? She knew trying to find Miss Simon's home number was hopeless. Could Miss Simon have a home at all? And supposing she did, in which

borough—Queens? Brooklyn? Staten Island? Karen
cracked the door of the phone booth in time to hear the
smooth, British loudspeaker voice booming out:

"Passengers for BOAC Flight ny-un-oh-ny-un for
London are requested to proceed to the departure
lounge at once for pre-boarding check-in and seat
assignment. Passengers for BOAC Flight ny-un-oh-
ny . . ."

Karen gathered up her carryall and hung her purse
on her shoulder. She buttoned up her long winter coat
to the neck and started off, feeling the damp March
winds of London swirling around her already. This
morning she had been in Miss Sands's English class.
Tomorrow she'd be in England. A little thrill of fear
went through her, along with a twitch of excitement.

3

For years, whenever Karen was somewhere between sleep and waking, she'd have the dream. Not a dream, exactly, because she could control it, think it through. More of a memory. It began with the big house on a rise above the lake. Three brilliant colors: the green of the hill, the flat blue water, and the white house standing against white clouds.

It was the place at Lake Geneva, Wisconsin, where they'd spent the summer she was nine. She and the housekeeper stayed there all season long, and Dad flew in for weekends as often as he could. She'd still been too young to wonder why they were there, a thousand miles from New York. But she'd loved it and loved remembering it. Swimming off the pier and watching for the little boat that nosed around Conference Point bringing the mail. And the other houses, old and solid with long porches and striped awnings. They were all summer people, but it was nearly like a neighborhood. Nearly like normal life.

The family staying next door—through the iron fence and the rose garden—were the Fieldings from Libertyville, Illinois. Their son Jay was eleven. He tried to drown Karen in the bird bath before they became buddies. At the end of the summer, just to round off the season, she'd turned the garden hose on him when he was dressed up in white slacks and a new, adult-looking blazer.

Sometime in between, he'd overcome his prejudice against girls. They'd belly-flopped in deep water, woven an endless stinkweed chain, and played Monopoly with fake money that the lake breeze sent whirling. Once they'd run off all the way to Williams Bay on the shore path. They'd bought Hostess cupcakes and a pair of underwater goggles and were brought home in a police car.

"Are you rich?" Jay had asked her one day in the covered swing.

"I don't know," she'd said. "How much is it?"

"A lot. My mother owns seven drugstores and my dad has implement factories."

"My mother's dead."

"I know. I'm not supposed to mention it. But do you suppose you're rich anyway?"

"I guess so, but I can't have anything I want."

"What do you want you can't have?"

"I don't know."

And Jay had told her, a hundred times, how he was going to go away to boarding school when he was thirteen. It had impressed her mightily then. But that was before she knew she'd be going away to school, too. Jay, the little boy who seemed so big to her then, with his hair bleached to straw by the August sun.

They'd tried to keep in touch after that summer. But later he'd gone to England to school—to Eton— and finally she didn't hear from him again. And she'd write to him those letters she never mailed.

To England. Karen opened her eyes. She was wide awake. The pillow behind her head had slipped down under the seat. It was daylight outside the plane window. She could see the end of the wing.

Jay was in England, as far as she knew. She tried to replace the image of a little soprano-voice boy with the eighteen-year-old he was now. It was no use trying. He remained an eleven-year-old in her mind. It had all been too long ago, too far away.

Still, the thought of him pleased her. She felt in her purse for the note from Miss Simon with the names of strangers, Mr. and Mrs. Sydney Sutton.

The stewardess came down the aisle, checking on the sleeping passengers. She looked alert with her useless little cap at a jaunty angle. But her smile seemed forced, and she nodded a little too brightly.

Karen checked her watch. It was just after two in the morning. Yet it was daylight. They were flying toward the clouded sunrise, meeting it halfway. She moved the hands ahead. Seven in the morning, European time, with only a sliver of night between yesterday and today. Unreal.

The smell of hot coffee drifted back from the galley. Karen decided to stretch her legs and throw cold water at her morning face before breakfast. She slid across the two empty seats beside her and stood up in the aisle. But the stewardess was just behind her, blocking the way.

"I'm afraid I'll have to ask you to remain in your seat." Just at that moment the seat belt sign flashed on.

"Are we there already?" Karen asked her.

"Well, not exactly."

Karen had flown enough to recognize a nervous stewardess when she saw one. Sitting back down and clamping the seat belt, she looked out the window and searched for land. But there was nothing but cloud cover for miles below, layer after layer. She felt cold. Her hands trembled as she pulled a blanket over her knees.

"Good morning, ladies and gentlemen, the captain has asked me to interrupt your rest and offers his regrets for disturbing you." The loudspeaker voice was

heavily British and as smooth as honey. It belonged to
another stewardess. The one who had just spoken to
Karen was still in the aisle, gently jostling sleeping
forms.

"We ask you to extinguish all smoking materials and
to fasten your seat belts." There was a pause then. But
the voice continued in a higher key. "It will be necessary to make an unscheduled landing in approxi-
mately twenty minutes." This announcement jolted
the rest of the dozing passengers awake. Heads
popped up all along the half-empty plane. "We will be
landing at Shannon International Airport in Ireland,
and there will be a short delay."

The loudspeaker crackled and seemed to go dead.
Several of the passengers turned to the stewardess in
the aisle. Her face was a careful zero. But the speaker
system came on again, louder. "In order to comply
with international safety regulations, the captain has
asked us to review with you the procedures governing
emergency landings." The word *emergency* leaped out
of the announcement and swept through the cabin.

Somewhere ahead of Karen's seat a woman's shrill
voice said, "What is it? What's happening?"

"Kindly remove any pens, pencils, or any sharp objects from your persons. Make certain that all fold-
down trays are in the upright position and firmly se-
cured. Place all objects, including handbags, beneath
your seats, put on your coats, and remove your shoes."

"My shoes?" The shrill voice ahead of Karen rang
out. "*My shoes?*" Karen slipped out of hers automatically, arranging them neatly with her toes. How important it was to line up her shoes carefully, she
thought vaguely. If everyone follows directions to the
letter, nothing bad will happen. The plane's engines
droned on evenly. Everyone seemed to be in the same
eerie silence between forced calm and stunned terror.

The stewardess moved quickly up the aisle, pulling

the coats out of the overhead racks. Fur, tweed, and camel's hair cascaded down on passengers bending over to take off their shoes. It was a moment too busy for panic.

"We draw your attention once again to the emergency exits on either side of the main cabin." The stewardess dropped the last coat and pointed out the doors. Somewhere near the front of the cabin she reached down and picked up a baby and carried him back down the aisle, everyone's eyes on her.

"It is unlikely that we will be employing these exits. However, to facilitate immediate deplaning once we have landed, we will be using the rear exit door. Exit from the craft will be by means of an emergency chute for maximum speed and efficiency. Very small children will be assisted by the flight attendants."

"Are we over land?" the same woman's hysterical voice pierced the cabin, asking the question in everyone's mind. "Are we over la—"

The loudspeaker voice continued, "We anticipate a routine landing at Shannon. We remind you, as always, to remain in your seats until the plane has come to a complete halt. You will be directed by the flight attendants concerning use of the emergency—"

The plane banked sharply. There was the sound of a pile of trays collapsing in the galley. Karen was torn between burying her face in her hands and staring out the window. The plane was making a sharp turn. Suddenly she was looking almost straight down along the line of the wing. The clouds parted, and land lay below. The green fields and stone walls of Ireland. It'll be all right now, whatever it is, she said almost aloud. Then she saw the firetrucks.

The plane was in a tight pattern now, negotiating a figure eight. Karen was suddenly on the high side, staring up into clouds, absolutely alone for a moment on the highest hill of a roller coaster. The silence in the plane was complete except for the baby murmuring in the stewardess's arms.

Then they were straightening out and losing altitude. The engines roared on normally. Karen stared at her toes. Dad, she thought, I wish Dad . . .

The wheels touched down smoothly. The level line of the world swept past the wingtip as the motors reversed and whined. Her seat belt strained against Karen's stomach. The plane rolled to a stop just as the speaker system found its voice again.

"Ladies and gentlemen, kindly remain in your seats. Passengers located in the rear of the aircraft will deplane first on instructions from the flight attendant. Please leave all luggage, handbags, and other parcels at your seat. Carry only your shoes."

A gale of cold air swept up the aisle as the rear door was opened. There was a terrifying hissing sound, like a monster at the door. "Ladies and gentlemen, the sound you now hear is the inflation of the emergency chute."

Karen sat still and obedient. Being out of the sky was only half a relief. Her toes itched to feel the earth itself. She forced her mind completely away from the fire trucks. Somewhere behind her the long yellow emergency chute was inflating like an elongated life raft. Then, moments later, the stewardess was beside her. "Now," she said. Karen started up. "Take your shoes." She walked part way back, to the end of the line of silent passengers. A tiny old woman she hadn't even seen before was standing very straight in front of her. She carried a large Macy's shopping bag in one hand and her lace-up shoes in the other.

Karen looked farther ahead to see another stewardess in the open doorway sending passangers down the chute, like tobogganers. They were peeling out the door at very close intervals. "No, madam, you may *not* deplane with that shopping bag!"

"But I shall need the contents of it!"

"Madam, I'm *sorry*!" The shopping bag was whisked out of the old lady's hand, and she slipped down the billowing chute, legs high and flailing. Two men on the ground at the other end were stationed to catch her. Then it was Karen's turn. She heard the soft scream of the nylon chute against her wool coat. In the next second, strong arms were planting her on her feet and pushing her forward, out of the path of the next passenger. Like a playground slide, she thought, and broke into a run.

There was a fire engine in the middle distance, and beyond it ambulances. All the passengers were running in a disciplined sort of Indian file. For the first time Karen felt real panic, as if the plane had turned into something too terrible to look back at. Like the city in the Bible.

Past the fire truck, the runners were gathered into a group. Uniformed airport workers were assisting in the roundup. A red-cheeked girl in an Irish Airlines uniform stepped briskly up. "All right now, miss, just this way."

Karen looked around for the first time, at a flat and empty landscape. "But where's the airport?"

"Ah, 'tis well away from here. You'll be going in by bus."

"But why are we way out at the end of the runway?"

"And where would you be with a bomb threat? You'd not have the airport *and* great duty-free shop blown to cinders, would you?"

"Bomb threat?"

"The same. And entirely too many of them these days if someone should ask me. As if the Irish hadn't troubles enough of our own! You might like to put on your shoes now. And welcome to Ireland!"

4

The ambulances were empty. Behind them a bus was filling up with passengers from the plane. Everyone appeared to burst into words at the same time. "What in the world is going on here?" "Must be a bomb threat." "I'm supposed to connect with a flight to Geneva." "The plane seemed all right; a bomb threat, undoubtedly." "My cosmetic bag is still on that awful plane." "What could it be but a bomb threat; with a skyjacking we'd certainly have known, wouldn't we?"

The last of the travelers were clambering aboard, with flapping shoelaces and red, puffing faces. Two overage hippies at the front of the bus were giggling out of control. "Is this like some kind of a wild scene or what?"

A ripple of hilarity worked through them all. In another minute, Karen thought, we'll be screaming with insane laughter. But the red-cheeked Irish Airlines girl in the green uniform stepped firmly up into the bus. She nodded at the driver.

In an oddly routine voice she said, "Good morning, ladies and gentlemen, I'm Miss Kinsella, welcoming you warmly to Shannon, though I know it's not the destination you're after choosing yourselves. Your plane has received a bomb threat, and the news of it was radioed ahead from New York."

There was a general murmur in the bus, almost of

satisfaction. "Experience has taught us that most such threats are false alarms, someone acting a bit naughty. But I've no doubt you will appreciate that we take no chances.

"Our demolition squad—the finest in Europe—has already begun its investigations." The bus ground into gear and started off toward the distant terminal buildings. "Your luggage will be transferred to a new aircraft as soon as the investigations are complete and the baggage is shifted. You'll be able to continue your journey on to London with no further delay."

The waiting room where they were gathered was well away from the main terminal. It was a no-man's-land with faulty fluorescent lights that blinked and dimmed. A grouchy-looking businessman was pacing up and down before the foggy window, muttering, "I oughta be in London right now. I oughta be—"

So should I, Karen thought, staring down into the steam from a mug of milky tea. She imagined that she saw in it two faceless figures, her mother's cousins. The Suttons. She wondered what they were like, what they looked like. But their faces were pale empty circles. They'll be worried, she thought. And suddenly she was almost eager to get on a plane again to continue this unlikely trip. Maybe the Suttons will have heard from Dad. Maybe they remember Mother.

There were rumors of breakfast, but none appeared. The airline people bustled through the room, and telephones rang in the distance. Down the bench from Karen, the baby's mother was changing him with diapers provided by Irish Airlines. "He could do with a bottle," the mother said, vaguely in Karen's direction. But the baby only purred and bubbled.

There was an announcement that their luggage had been transferred to another plane. A general sigh went up as everyone stopped listening for a muffled explosion at the far end of the runway. Then, later, they were instructed to put on their coats and be ready to leave. But it was a false alarm. Noon came and went.

At last, they were standing outside in a group, cheering as a new plane lumbered toward them. Miss Kinsella was capably holding them back as the plane drew to a stop in a blast of cold air and noise. Portable stairs were rolled out from somewhere, and the plane's door opened.

Everyone edged forward automatically, but Miss Kinsella held her ground. She looked proof against a cattle stampede. It was at that moment Karen felt a hand on her arm. She turned to look up into the face of a man she'd never seen before. He was wearing a trench coat and anchoring his hat with his free hand.

"Miss Karen Beatty?" he said to her. It came as a whisper over the roar of the plane. "Miss Beatty?" He began to pull her aside. He was standing so near that nobody would notice what he was doing. Instinctively, she tried to pull away.

"You're not a passenger, are you?" she said.

"I beg your pardon?" His grip on her arm tightened, painfully. She tried to pull away. Everyone else was looking in the direction of the plane.

"Are you with the airlines?" she said.

"The airlines? Oh, yes. Step this way please." Karen stood frozen. If it weren't for his hand gripping her arm, she would have walked away with him. But . . .

"Glad to have had you in Ireland. Come again when you can make a proper stay!" Miss Kinsella was able to make herself heard above everything. The passengers surged forward toward the plane's stairsteps.

"Miss Beatty—Karen—you're supposed to come with me. I've been sent to—"

Karen wrenched her arm away from him and panicked suddenly, perhaps too late. The other passengers had moved ahead. When she tried to take a step away, she was facing Miss Kinsella, who was staring past her at the man in the trench coat.

"Here now," she said, and started forward. "What's all this?" Karen felt his hand loosen and slip away. She turned back then and saw him running across the tarmac toward the main terminal. "Here now," Miss Kinsella yelled after him. But he was well away. Karen watched him into the distance. Then she turned, and ran toward the London plane.

They were over the Irish Sea, and lunch was being served at last. It had taken the first airborne half-hour to sort out and redistribute the piles of purses, brief cases, and shopping bags that had been heaped into the new plane. A big woman in a fur coat wandered up the aisle, saying, "I've found everything but my Pucci scarf. Anybody see a Pucci scarf? It's marked *Pucci*."

Karen touched the red marks on her arm where the man had gripped her through her coat. She felt numb, except for her heart that throbbed just a little faster than the rhythm of the plane motors. It was too much. Right from the beginning until now. Who was the man in the trench coat? And what did he want? And how did he know her name? She tried to sort through everything. She was used to thinking things out on her own. But nothing like this.

The man. What did he look like? Could she identify him again? She tried to remember the fragment of face between his coat collar and the brim of his hat. A blank. Another blank, like the Suttons. She felt surrounded by faceless strangers. Not like the first day at a new school. Not a bit like that. In a half hour, she'd be meeting the Suttons, if all went well. If all went well. What more could happen? She almost began to long for those stranger-cousins.

Someone had left a New York newspaper in the seat

pocket ahead of her. She pulled it out and tried to
read it, to make some kind of contact with the sane
world. But her eyes scanned, then skipped. She
couldn't seem to get beyond the meaningless head-
lines: MANAGEMENT QUESTIONS STRIKERS'
SINCERITY—METROPOLITAN MUSEUM BUYS
PRIZE GREEK VASE—MAN SET ON FIRE BY UN-
KNOWN ENEMIES.

It was all too remote. New York was too far away,
back in some distant world, along with the Isobel Kelvin Academy, the hard frosted Connecticut hills, and
everything she'd ever known.

The plane swept in a great arc over London. The
Thames wound below, divided into segments by the
bridges. She looked for Big Ben and saw only
skyscrapers. Great high-rise complexes. "Europe," she
whispered, but it was no more real than a map. Nothing was but the marks on her arm that were shading
from red to blue.

There was a round of applause from the passengers
when the plane touched down. All the fear and the
delay were re-forming into An Experience to tell the
folks back home. Karen could hear some of the lame
jokes the other travelers were trying out on each
other. "How did you find Ireland?" "Oh, it was just
right there at the end of the chute." "Well, what did
you think of Ireland?" "Oh, it's a lot like Cuba."

They filed out of the plane and along an unending
network of corridors. Beyond the luggage-claim room,
two lines were forming at what looked like supermar-
ket check-out counters. One was labeled "British Pass-
ports"; the other, "Aliens."

The Aliens line edged slowly forward. Karen slid
her big suitcase along beside her and tried to juggle
her purse and carryall while keeping her passport
ready.

She was almost up to the customs officer when she saw a wide doorway farther ahead. It was jammed with people meeting their friends and men who held up signs that read, "Taxis for All London Hotels."

"Good afternoon, miss. May I see your passport please? What is the purpose of your stay in the United Kingdom?"

"Just a visit—with relatives." Karen looked past the customs man, wondering how she could identify the Suttons once she she got to them.

"Do you have in your possesion any liquids or drugs or any gifts for any person in the United-Kingdom?"

"What? Oh, no. Nothing." With her feet on the ground at last, Karen was almost staggering with fatigue. She would have gladly stretched out on the customs counter and gone into a very private, very restful coma.

"And are you traveling alone?"

"Yes. I'm alone."

The rubber stamp struck the first blank page of her passport. "Thank you, miss. Enjoy your visit. Next please!"

They weren't hard to recognize, somehow. Maybe that's the way with long-lost families, Karen thought. Two people, standing together, closely watching each new arrival through the door. Older than she'd expected, middle-aged. Why does the word *cousins* always suggest children? Karen wondered through her haze.

"Karen, darling!" Mrs. Sutton rushed forward. "You are Karen, aren't you? Of course you are! Syd! help the child with her case! My dear, you've no idea what a state we've been in! Whatever happened on that wretched plane? Of course, they told us *nothing!* You must have been *terrified!* Oh, my dear, how glad we are to have you with us."

She drew Karen gently to her and held her for a moment. Tears brimmed in Karen's eyes. They were inevitable, but she worked hard to keep them back. What a relief, she thought. What a relief.

"And this is my husband, Syd."

He took her hand in both of his. "We're glad to have you at last, my girl." And looked straight across at her, his eyes twinkling He was just a fraction of an inch shorter than his wife.

"And now, my dears, we've had *quite enough* of airports and airplanes for one day's adventuring!" Mrs. Sutton linked arms with Karen and waved Syd into action. They swept off on the tide of people, out into the gray and chilly afternoon.

Mrs. Sutton reminded Karen of some faintly birdlike creature. There were feathers on her very English hat, for one thing. And her head bobbed in time to her steady conversation. She had a heart-shaped face under the feathers and a sprinkling of freckles amid the wrinkles.

In all the tangle of taxis and double-decker BOAC buses, there was one black car waiting. Mrs. Sutton made straight for it. A very large young man in a gray suit jumped out and opened the rear door. "Karen, this is Albert." He hung his big head and swung her luggage away, all of it in one hand.

He might be anybody from their chauffeur to their son, Karen thought. But it wasn't a time for solving riddles. Too many hours, too many miles since she'd slept. Words, faces, England, came and went.

And suddenly they were humming along a highway with Albert at the wheel. On the wrong side of the road of course. Karen tried to focus on the rows of brick houses with orange tiled roofs, bristling with television antennas. "She's very like Eleanor, don't you think so, Syd?"

Eleanor? Karen tried to concentrate. Her mother.

Eleanor. "Now, Blanche, you know I never knew
Eleanor. I didn't even know you in those days."

"Oh, of course you didn't. But you've seen pictures
of Eleanor often enough. There's that snap somewhere taken of her and me together on the seafront at
Brighton. Right at the end of the war, it was. Why it
might be Karen herself." And then she squeezed Kar-
en's arm. "Your mother was the pretty one, of course,
and I see her in you. It's quite like old times really."

Karen must have dozed, because the car was
threading its way through city traffic. There was a
flash of color from a street corner flower stand, a little
spring explosion in the gray day. They turned into a
quieter street walled in by tall, cream-colored houses
with high stoops. There were trees at the end of the
street as it opened into a long rectangle of gleaming
houses stretching into the distance on either side of a
narrow park. Cornwall Gardens, Karen thought, and
tried to look alive.

73A was exactly like its row of towering neighbors.
Steep steps up to a tiny porch with a brass bell plate
polished to a mirror. Then the door opened, and a
large woman filled the space. Her hair was a mop of
gray fuzz, and she wore an apron over her vast print
dress. She stared down at them. "Ah, Mrs. Plasket,"
Blanche Sutton said to her, "here we are at long last,
fainting for a nice cup of tea!"

The tea was ready, laid in the dark drawing room.
Mrs. Plasket withdrew silently. Albert clumped along
the hall and up the stairs carrying Karen's luggage.
She yearned to follow her suitcase and collapse in a
room of her own, but there was the ritual of tea first.
The real England, finally. "Now, my dear, tell us absolutely everything about that rather extraordinary
plane trip."

And Karen began. The tea fanned just enough life
into her to get her started. When she came to the part

about sliding down the chute at Shannon, both the Suttons stared in horrified amazement. Blanche urged her on with sharp little bobs of her head.

But Karen was drooping again, losing the thread of the story. Absent-mindedly she rubbed the bruises on her arm where the mystery man had gripped her. "But, Karen, my dear, you've ever such a nasty bruise on your left arm there. Did that happen when you had to slide down the chute?"

"What?" Karen said. "Oh, this? Yes, I guess it must have."

5

Daylight and darkness seemed to come at random intervals. After a dreamless, exhausted sleep, Karen opened her eyes to morning and an unfamiliar ceiling. Instead of the acoustical tiles of the Isobel Kelvin Academy dorm, there were small, misshapen cherubs frozen around a light fixture with tulip-shaped shades. The ceiling was so high she seemed to be lying at the bottom of a well.

"I suppose," she said out loud, "it's tomorrow instead of yesterday."

"Yes, miss." The voice came from the doorway. Mrs. Plasket stood there with a breakfast tray. She advanced. "You'll want a good English breakfast," she announced, turning her broad beam away from Karen and setting down the tray on a little table. It was clear that Mrs. Plasket didn't approve of breakfast in bed. Or small talk. She marched out of the room.

There was a sink behind a screen in the far corner. Both taps offered cold water. Karen had found the bathroom down the hall last night, but she'd only have to find it all over again this morning. And the floor was too cold.

Someone had unpacked for her, so she started through the room, checking for her brush in all the drawers and cupboards. Most of them were empty. The brush was in the last possible place, and she spent fifteen busy minutes on her hair, straining to see

herself in the murky little mirror over the sink. My
hair was beginning to look like Mrs. Plasket's, she said
to spur herself on.

The mirror reflected the corner of a window. She
turned to look out at London. But it was a rear view
down to a narrow courtyard. Once there'd been an
oval lily pond, but it was paved with dead leaves. The
view ended almost before it began with a high back
wall.

The toast was stone cold in the rack. Under a metal
cover were eggs and—Karen stared—fish with their
heads still on. She replaced the cover with a bang.
Then took it off again. She didn't dare not eat a good
English breakfast. Mrs. Plasket would be back for the
tray.

Downstairs, the house looked deserted. The drawing-
room fireplace was cold and swept. The room had
an unlived-in look, except for an impressive television
set, surrounded by ancient, overpowering furniture.
Everything had been very elegant once, Karen
thought. By the long front windows there was a grand
piano with a silver-framed picture on it.

It seemed more than likely that she and Mrs. Plasket were alone in the house. She turned back to the
hall and saw her coat hanging on a hook. She wanted
to talk to Cousin Blanche. The questions were rising
in her again after a night's sleep. About Dad, and
other things, farther back. About Mother. Instead, she
put on her coat and slipped quietly out of the house.

London at last, Karen thought, drawn by the boom
of the city beyond the leafy square. Past Grenville
Place she could see a major cross street streaming
with boxy cabs and top-heavy buses. I'd better not go
too far, she thought, just up the busy street and along
it for a while.

It was called Gloucester Road, full of life and color,
a perfect contrast to Mrs. Plasket's breakfast. The lit-

tle shops were bulging with enticements, but the prices were baffling: pounds and new pence. An intriguing old-new world. Even the throngs on the sidewalk seemed less faceless than other crowds, friendly and almost familiar. Maybe my mother shopped along this street once, she thought.

Ahead, Gloucester Road entered a park, as green as springtime. Karen turned back then to retrace her steps. They might wonder where she was. Besides, this is England, and it might rain any minute. She was the only stroller in sight without an umbrella. Most of the men wore trench coats. She remembered the man with the steely grip and the trench coat then. Well, it had obviously been the perfect disguise. The thought of him nagged at her.

She'd almost walked past a little branch post office without noticing it. Not that she'd consciously been looking for it. She went in. "Good morning, love." The voice came from behind a little barred window.

Karen was surprised at what she heard herself asking: "Ah—could you tell me how I could send a letter to a boy at Eton?"

"The school, you mean?"

"Yes."

"Well, Eton is in the town of Eton, but the post office is Windsor. Do you know your friend's house?"

"His house?"

"That's right. You see the young gentlemen at Eton all live in residences called houses."

"Would you have to know the house to send a letter there?"

"Oh no, I shouldn't think so, love. Just Eton College, Windsor, will do nicely. And it's not far off, you know. Only an hour in the train. But then you're thinking of posting a letter, aren't you? Do you need stamps?"

"Yes," Karen said. "I mean no. I came out without any money. I'll stop back. Thank you."

She hurried back to Cornwall Gardens then, thinking about Jay, wondering if she'd really taken a step closer to him. And then wondering if he'd even remember her.

The front door was standing open. Even before she started inside, she heard voices in the hall. Cousin Blanche's voice angry. "Really, Mrs. Plasket, I'm quite, *quite* appalled. Letting that child walk straight out of the house and—"

"It's nothing to do with me, I'm sure, Mrs. Sutton. I have me work to do and plenty of it."

"Karen! Oh thank heaven! We hardly knew what to think. I was just saying to Mrs. Plasket—Oh, but never mind, here you are. My dear, you might have been swallowed up in London and gone without a trace!" Cousin Blanche threw her arms around Karen as if she was making sure she was really there.

"I was just doing a little neighborhood sightseeing," Karen said. After too many years of independence, Karen felt a little smothered by all this maternal concern for her whereabouts.

"Yes, of course you were. And I must say it's warmer outside than in this great tomb of a house. Mrs. Plasket, couldn't we have a fire laid in the drawing room?"

"Seems quite comfortable enough to me," Mrs. Plasket mumbled, "but then of course I've me work to do."

"Mrs. Plasket, *please.*"

Mrs. Plasket built up a hot fire with cool efficiency. It was time for what Cousin Blanche called "elevenses"—mid-morning coffee and sweet biscuits. Mrs. Plasket vanished and returned with a tray bearing a somewhat dented silver coffee pot. The biscuit plate was cracked across. "There were the best I could find. I'm—"

"That will do nicely, Mrs. Plasket. Thank you," Cousin Blanche said hastily. And as soon as Mrs. Plasket had left again, Cousin Blanche moved the coffee table back from the fireplace. "I do believe she's trying to smoke us out. Now, my dear, tell me every place you've been this morning and everything you've seen."

This just won't do, Karen thought. I should be asking the questions, if I can manage to break in. "Oh, I didn't get very far, Mrs. Su—"

"Oh, call me Blanche, dear. Even if I am amply old enough to be your mother. We stand on no ceremony in this house."

"Well, to tell the truth, I'm wondering what I'm doing here. I mean I'm glad to be here, but—"

"Shall I tell you a secret?" Blanche said with her head on one side. "I'm wondering too! I said to Syd when we heard, 'Syd, after all these years!' And here you are, practically grown up."

Karen decided Blanche was off the track again, but she dropped her voice suddenly and said, "Karen, I really don't know what to make of it. After all these years and very little contact—none, really. I think, Karen, your father is having some trouble. And he wants you to be safe. And so he thought of us. I hope it isn't serious, and I hope it will pass. But I can't help being pleased that he did think of us. You know, Karen, whatever has happened, you're the most important person in the world to him, the most precious."

"I've never been sure of that," Karen said.

"I think you can be sure of it now."

"But what kind of trouble could he be in!" Karen said that night after Syd had come home from work. They were at the dining room table, having a Good English Dinner, silently served by Mrs. Plasket.

"Oh, I shouldn't worry about it if I were you. You're much too young to bear all the troubles of the world." Syd helped himself to another serving of tough little Brussels sprouts and poured brown gravy over them.

Blanche bobbed her head forcefully in his direction. "Syd, sometimes I think you're beginning to lose your vision. If you will as much as cast a gaze across the table, you'll see that Karen is no longer a child. I think it would have been a very good idea indeed if Steve—your father, dear"—Blanche bobbed once toward Karen—"if Steve had been able to spend a great deal more time with Karen after poor Eleanor died. And I do think it would have been wise of him to keep her informed about his comings and goings and his business. Men!" Blanche tapped the tablecloth with one emphatic finger. "As far as they're concerned, their wives are eternal featherheads and their daughters are forever moppets. I shudder to think what sort of father *you* would have made, Syd. I *really* do."

That jolted Karen into a smile. "Well, that's one mystery solved anyway."

"Whatever do you mean, my dear?"

"Well, I wasn't quite sure about Albert when I met him yesterday. I thought maybe he was—"

Blanche erupted into laughter, "You never!" Syd's knife went clattering down on his plate. "Now you mention it, of course," Blanche said through her mirth, "he does look just the least bit like Syd. I never thought—"

"Oh, give over, Blanche!" Syd said, vastly less amused. "In point of fact, Karen, he's one of Blanche's lame ducks, is Albert."

"He's nothing of the sort," Blanche said, pulling herself together. "If anything, he's your protege. Actually, Karen, Albert's a boy—well, hardly a boy now—but he was a boy from the East End, down by the docks, you know. He started by doing odd jobs for us, and I suppose we're a bit of family for him. And we rather look after one another, though he comes and goes as he pleases."

Karen settled back in her chair, tasting the flavor of a family, laughing and talking in the pool of light above the table in the otherwise gloomy room. She felt herself settling in. The school girl she'd been two days before was already beginning to fade. When Dad gets here, she thought, everything will be fine.

Mrs. Plasket was clearing away the plates, moving in the darkness just outside the circle of light. Her face came and went as she leaned forward to retrieve something from the table. Karen looked up at her. Mrs. Plasket's eyes were fixed on her, steadily, just for a moment. But the moment seemed to linger. Mrs. Plasket doesn't belong, it occurred to her suddenly, and then she wondered why she thought it.

6

The rest of the week slipped by. Syd was no sooner off to some office in the City in the mornings than Blanche went into action planning the days' events, showing Karen "a bit of London." She was very long on shopping and very short on museums, Karen noticed.

They'd take the "tube" from the Gloucester Road Underground Station and emerge at Hyde Park Corner. From there they'd work their way down Piccadilly and up the curve of Regent Street. Karen wouldn't have minded a trip or two down King's Road, Chelsea, for the boutiques. But Blanche's taste was firmly fixed somewhere in the late 1940's. She cooed over sweater sets in the Burlington Arcade and silk scarves at Liberty's. They always finished up with a late lunch in some ladies' tea room atop a department store. It was all very civilized and matronly. Karen couldn't decide if she was growing up in London or growing old with Blanche.

She'd wanted to open the checking account at the bank, according to Miss Simon's instructions. No word yet from her father, and no telling how much longer she'd have to wait. But Blanche wouldn't hear of any talk about money. "You're our guest, my dear. And we won't have you spending a penny of your own. When I think of all the good times Eleanor and I used to have together, well, having you here is like having her back."

The three of them had their after-dinner coffee every evening in the drawing room. One night Karen found herself gazing at the picture on the grand piano that apparently nobody played. She walked over to look at it more closely. A little girl sitting with one leg tucked under, smiling into the camera. She had the Dutch bob and the starched smock of the early 1930's.

"I wondered when you'd take notice of that. You've seen a print of it before, I shouldn't wonder," Blanche said.

"No, where would I have seen it?" But suddenly she knew it must have been her mother. A solemn little English girl who'd been told to sit very still.

"What was she like?"

"At that age? Oh, I don't know really. Our mothers were sisters, you see, but they didn't get on. Then Eleanor's mother died—your grandmother—and later my mother was killed in the Blitz. By then we were nearly grown, Eleanor and I, and we drifted together. The war was a terrible thing. Wasn't it, Syd?"

"Um?"

"Oh, never mind. Syd was in the army the whole time, out in India."

"Burma."

"Yes, Burma. But I will say, bad as it was, we were all young then and managed to have our bit of fun. Eleanor and I stayed in London through the thick of it. And of course if it hadn't been for the war and the Americans staying on over here afterwards, she'd never have met your father. He promised her the moon and swept her away. Terribly romantic."

It sounded like an old movie on TV, Karen thought. There used to be a picture at home of her father and mother on their wedding day, he in his Air Force uniform, she with dark lipstick and padded shoulders.

Karen tried to put the pieces together, but her mother was still mostly a collage of old photographs and the elusive scent of lavender.

And, when she came to think of it, did she know her father any better?

Karen stared into the fire and the thought of him swept over her. She was getting along fine, of course. She always had. She'd learned her lessons in independence thoroughly. And yet maybe he needed her. For the first time in their lives. While she was sipping tea with Blanche in genteel London, maybe he was . . .

She was tired suddenly, and footsore from those shopping expeditions. She started up to bed, but turned to say to Blanche and Syd, "Maybe we ought to be doing simething."

They seemed to know what she meant, Blanche at least. "I wish we could. But we don't know where he is."

"No," Karen said, "but maybe Miss Simon—"

"Oh, your father's secretary?"

"Yes. How did you know?"

"The cablegram came from her. The one telling us you were on your way and that your father would get in touch with you here, you know."

No, she hadn't known. She'd thought Dad had contacted the Suttons himself. It made him seem even more remote.

Miss Simon. Everything seemed to start from her, Dad's efficient and reliable right arm. But what if she'd stopped playing that role and had taken on another one? Not so efficient, not so reliable?

Her head buzzed, and she said a quick goodnight. The hallway was dark, but she knew the stairs by now. She started up them, with words ringing in her ears. Judy's at Grand Central Station . . . "Simon has everything on a minute-by-minute schedule . . ."

"When you get to the airport, call her at the office . . ."

And another voice, echoing from farther back . . . "You look wonderful, sweetheart. But you're growing up . . ." And Bea's "Your dad could be doing time right now . . . right now . . . right now . . ."

And finally those words from the very end of childhood:

> ANDREAS DADDYS A FIREMAN
> CARMENS FATHERS A COOK
> RACHELS DAD IS A DOCTOR
> BUT KARENS OLD MAN IS A . . .

Karen stood unmoving on the stairs. She could feel the panic working in her throat, suddenly, before she could get her defenses up. And why now, at this moment? She tried to think her way out of the fear, the feeling, whatever it was.

But she couldn't take another step up into the darkness. She turned back and looked down toward the wedge of light from the drawing-room door.

The sounds her mind was making ebbed away. She could hear snatches of conversation between Blanche and Syd.

"She's worried," Blanche was saying.

Syd's voice rumbled in reply. He was harder to hear, ". . . up to you to keep her from worrying . . ."

Karen turned then and walked on up the stairs.

Before her hand found the doorknob, she knew somehow that there was someone in her room. Why this didn't send her fleeing in terror, she didn't know. Maybe she wasn't in a mood to trust her own mind. She turned the knob and walked straight in. The light was on, and Mrs. Plasket was turning down her bed. She looked around at Karen calmly and said, "Early night tonight, miss?"

"Yes, I guess I'm worn out."

Mrs. Plasket went over to the big wardrobe, took down Karen's robe and pajamas, and laid them out on the bed. It was the nightly routine, but on the other nights she'd stayed up later and had missed Mrs. Plasket. She wished she'd finish up and go. But Mrs. Plasket didn't hurry through her ritual for anybody. Now she was drawing the curtains.

"Tea up or down in the morning, miss?"

"Oh, I'll come downstairs for it." Karen was glad to have the choice. She hadn't enjoyed waking up to dawn confrontations with Mrs. Plasket's stony face.

"Mr. and Mrs. Sutton usually have their morning tea up in their room, don't they?" Chitchat with Mrs. Plasket seemed unlikely, but making a stab at it was better than standing around dumbly until she left.

"I wouldn't know about *usually*, miss." Mrs. Plasket paused then. As if she was almost but not quite ready to make her exit. "They've had their tea upstairs every morning this week is all I know."

"Why just this week?" Karen was beginning to wonder if this conversation was as trivial as it seemed. There was something odd hanging in the air. The old woman hesitated again. Her tasks were finished, and she was looking directly at Karen.

"Because, miss, I've only been with them this week. I'm temporary."

"Oh." Karen wondered if this was a piece of the puzzle slipping into place. And if so, what puzzle?

Mrs. Plasket started for the door. Her hand was reaching out to it, but she turned back.

"And another thing, miss. It's the same with the Suttons."

"What?"

"I mean it's the same with them as with me. They've only been here this week themselves. Rented the place furnished is what they did. But it's nothing to do with me. I have me work to do. Goodnight to you, miss."

7

Even without her parting shot, Mrs. Plasket's sudden
burst of conversation might have given Karen a sleepless night. But it had the opposite effect. She was in a
deep, dreamless sleep in five minutes, but awake
again before daylight. Wide awake. She reached out
from her comfortable nest of bed clothes to switch on
the light. The damp five A.M. air seemed to cling to
her bare arm. Then the room loomed up at her in the
sudden light.

She fished her wool bathrobe up from the floor and
draped it around her shoulders. But she couldn't quite
coax her feet out of their warm pocket at the end of
the bed.

Almost for the first time she looked around the
room, really looked at it. Everything had been so new
to her at first. Except for the eye-catching cherubs on
the ceiling, she hadn't really concentrated on her sur-
roundings. There was the big mahogany wardrobe
where her clothes were hanging: two hulking doors
with a broken latch and a space above for her suitcase. A scaled-down upholstered chair with linen
hand towels placed to protect the headrest and arms.
It was drawn up to the stiff little breakfast table. A
chest of drawers, empty of everything but her few
traveling possessions. And not so much as an extra

blanket besides. The screen with the panels of old taffeta and behind it the sink and mirror.

There was one picture—above her bed. She turned to examine it. A dim view of brown poppies. And, of course, the bed itself, flanked by lamp tables, like a hotel room.

Exactly like a hotel room. Guest rooms in people's homes might be impersonal. But this impersonal? These weren't Blanche and Syd's things. This wasn't their house. Or at least it hadn't been for long. She had that on Mrs. Plasket's firm authority.

But how firm was her authority? If she was a "temporary," what could she know about the Suttons? For that matter, what could they know about her?

The night before, Karen's worry about her father had flowered into fear. This morning the fear was still there. But now she was afraid for herself. These people, they were strangers to her. Blanche and Syd and Mrs. Plasket. Even the little girl in the pictures downstairs. Her Mother. They were all strangers. Not faceless, of course. Not like people you pass in the night. Not like the man in the trench coat. They had faces.

And that could make them more dangerous.

Rising hysteria again. Karen slipped out of bed and planted her bare feet on the floor. She didn't even look for the old beaded moccasins she used for bedroom slippers. The freezing floor was a good shock treatment.

She walked over to the window and parted the velvet curtains. She was more than ready for daylight. But the square of sky above the end of the courtyard was only a little pale.

There was a break in the straight line of the rear garden wall. A jagged ripple in the silhouette. With a little imagination, Karen thought, it could be an arm. It moved.

She dropped the curtain. Without thinking much,

she walked over and switched off the light. Then she moved back to the window. Just as she parted the curtain again, she saw a form hoisting itself up and over the wall. A man dropped down on his feet in the courtyard. He stood there a moment. Then he stretched his arms up and threw his head back. And yawned. He walked toward her then, skirting the invisible lily pond, and let himself into a door below her feet. There had been just enough light for an instant to see who he was. Albert.

She found her moccasins then. And a pair of high wool skiing socks. And the body stocking she'd bought for dance class and had brought for warmth. She started with these and dressed to face the icy rigors of her room. Then she sat down on the edge of her bed with a pad of writing paper.

The ball point started for the white page. But she stopped and loosened her hold on it slightly. She had the pen in a death grip, tight, but trembling. And only partly from the cold. She had to reason with herself a little before she'd be able to write.

There's something worse, Karen thought, than being in danger. And that's being in possible danger. Not being sure. Risking the wrong word to the wrong person. Showing suspicion, doubt . . . fear. A fear they might see, or sense. But above all, not keeping your guard up.

Her hand steadied enough then. On the other side of the velvet curtain morning was coming. She could make some plans in this little scrap of time.

Doing *something*, and doing it quietly seemed the important thing. Even if it was the long shot of the century. And if there was nothing to fear after all . . .

But she knew there was. She worked out her plan for the next half hour or so as carefully as a school fire drill. She'd write the letter. Slip downstairs early. Find

a stamp and an envelope in the drawing-room desk.
Address the envelope. No, that was no good. She'd get
out of the house—leave the lock off the door—and
walk to the corner. Then address the envelope there
and mail the letter at the "pillar box."

Going all the way to the Gloucester Road post office would take unnecessary time. With any luck,
she'd be back in the house before even Mrs. Plasket
was stirring. Considering the evidence, Mrs. Plasket
seemed a prime suspect. She didn't belong.

But all this meant a little quiet luck and tight
scheduling. Miss-Simon-type scheduling. It would
have to be a short letter.

Calmer now, she began it:*Dear Jay* . . .

Two letters for Jay Fielding lay in the unsorted
heap of mail. It had been dumped in the mud room of
Wykeham House, the home away from home for forty
Etonians.

It was an ancient stone house almost in the shadow
of Eton Chapel. Below it, the High Street wandered
away from the school and down to the river between
a double row of picturesque tailor shops and tea
rooms. By noon when the morning haze had lifted,
Windsor Castle stood in the distance across the
Thames like a fictional fortress from a medieval leg-
end.

The young gentlemen of Wykeham House were a
bewildering collection, the sons of bishops and bar-
ons, bankers and brewers: a whole gathering of ado-
lescent dukes, two or three young earls-to-be, and one
American from Libertyville, Illinois.

In the ten minutes before the noon bell announcing
"boys' dinner," one of the youngest members of Wykeham House burst through the front door. He was
thirteen, dressed in a black suit with pants legs that

flapped high above his ankles. His nose was running as it did throughout most of the winter. And he was panting after the dash from a tutorial session in Latin grammar. His name was Desmond Hoaresham-D'ark.

Luckily, he was well ahead of the other first-year boys for once. He dropped on his knees to start sorting through the mail. The one with a Saunton postmark was for him, from his grandmother in Devon. He jammed it deep into his pocket where it would lie unread for weeks. Scattering letters wildly over the tiles, he kept up the search.

Maybe there was no mail for Fielding, but Desmond was taking no chances. He was fairly vague about Latin grammar, but very careful when it came to Jay Fielding.

For two reasons. The official one was that he was on "boy call" to Fielding, a time-honored Eton tradition and a chief part of being in the first year. It was Desmond's solemn duty to carry up the coal for Fielding's grate, to make Fielding's bed, to shine Fielding's shoes, to keep Fielding's football gear in working order. And to deliver Fielding's mail into Fielding's hand before boys' dinner. Punctually. It was part of the system, which made it a tradition at least three hundred years old. Desmond wasn't strong on tradition, of course. But he did know that when he was a sixth-former like Fielding, some runny-nosed, miserable little blighter would be running errands for him.

The second reason was that Fielding was his own private hero, and Desmond worshiped him.

He took the stone stairs at a gallop and exploded through a door. "Two letters for you today, Fielding!" he announced in a cracking voice.

Jay was standing in front of the mirror, struggling with a white bow tie, his badge as a house captain. Desmond gazed up at Fielding's six-foot height: his checked trousers that fitted; his black tail coat with the black braid; the flower in his buttonhole. The whole magnificent uniform signifying that Fielding belonged to Sixth Form Select, Eton's highest honor.

"Look, Des, would you give me a hand with this tie? It takes an Englishman to get it right."

Desmond dropped the letters on the desk and approached his idol. *It takes an Englishman* Desmond felt a little lightheaded, but he attacked the bow tie with suddenly steady fingers. Maybe that was why Fielding was his hero. Any other Senior treated his "boy" like a worm—or worse. But not Fielding. Always a good word, never a complaint. Not to mention the privilege of being called *Des* instead of *Hoaresham-D'ark*.

Maybe it had something to do with being an American. It was Desmond's cloudy impression that all Americans were friendly and considerate, except for the tourists. But of course Fielding was more than that. Fielding was what Desmond wanted to be.

The tie was finally pulled into the form of a lavish white moth. Desmond had no more excuse for hanging around. Besides, Fielding would want to read his letters before dinner.

"What are your plans for the spring vac, Des?"

"Madeira again. Mummy—I mean my mother wanted to try it again. But my father says the food's too foreign and there's nothing to do but lie in the sun. They've gone, though, because my mother had her heart set on it. I'm flying down at the end of next week to join them."

"Sounds good to me."

"T'isn't all that bad actually," Desmond said in his most adult manner. "Better than going on holiday with my Grandmother Hoaresham. *She* still goes to Monte Carlo."

"What's on for dinner, do you know?"

"Shepherd's pie and jam sponge with fruit sauce, I think," Des said. It was a gentle hint. Desmond made a reluctant retreat, leaving Jay with his letters and two minutes to read them.

One of them had a London postmark. If Jay had taken a closer look, he'd have seen at a glance that it was addressed in a girl's handwriting. But the other one was from the States. An oversized envelope streaked with red, white, and blue bands. It demanded immediate attention, clamored for it.

As he read the letter, he could hear the boom of his father's voice.

LIBERTY FARMS
LIBERTYVILLE, ILLINOIS

Dear Son,

Well how's the perfect English gent? Say, boy, let me tell you right off the bat how proud your mother is of you! Passing those A-Level Exams and all that. Great stuff! And you know how your old man feels about it—I don't care what that fancy Eton education of yours cost, it was worth it to me. You've got one happy Old Man on your hands, son!

And I'd like to see Harvard try to turn you down with a record like that! It isn't every day they have a chance for an Eton man anyway! So don't worry about an acceptance there. As I've told you before, I had a word with a friend of mine at the club who is a Pretty Big Harvard alum (Class of '53, I think) so we've got a lot going for us, and you can leave the worrying now to your Old Man.

Of course you know what your mother's like. She thinks you've been far enough away for too many years as it is. So she'd like to see you closer to home and keeps at me to get you into Northwestern. But I think the two of us can handle her if we put up a United Front.

And speaking of family get-togethers, your mother and I are throwing things into suitcases right now. We're coming over to London. I've got to see some men about some machinery. And I couldn't get away without bringing your mother ha ha. She's counting the hours till she can see her boy and you better believe it!

We're both sorry as we can be that we can't come over during your spring vacation and spend some real time with you. But this has to be a quicky trip and "strictly business" to keep my tax man happy.

We're stopping over in New York. I want to pay a call down on Wall Street to find out how they're throwing my money away (!) And you know what your mother's like. She has to get in a few hours of shopping. What with your inflation over there in Old England, she figures she can do about as well in New York pricewise.

Well, son, we'll be staying at the Doncaster in London, as usual, and we want to see as much of you as . . .

The bell for dinner had already sounded. His father's letter had the usual numbing effect on Jay, a mixture of gratitude and exasperation that somehow canceled each other out. Only it was worse this time than ever before. He hadn't planned on facing his parents until summer when he went home to Libertyville. He'd thought he had a few months more before the inevitable explosion. But now he'd have to face them sooner. Almost at once.

Today is Friday. Jay's eyes flicked to his desk calendar and back to the end of the letter. They'll be at the Doncaster Sunday. Two days away. Two days until he'd have to tell them he wasn't going to be entering Harvard—or Northwestern. Or taking any of the paths they were so ready to choose for him.

With all this ringing in his mind, he jammed his father's letter into his coat pocket along with the one with the London postmark. He was late already, a poor example to the younger students. Before he even started down the time-worn steps, he could visualize the slightly pained expression on his house tutor's face.

Desmond Hoaresham-D'ark had been optimistic. Instead of shepherd's pie, boys' dinner was featuring "bangers and mash" along with boiled cabbage. The three aromas mingled and rose up the stairs that Jay was heading down, two at a time. He made a smooth but speedy entrance into the dining hall. Desmond's eyes were upon him from one of the tables far down the room. Jay was at high table this week. He bobbed his head in the little ritual regret at the house tutor before settling into his seat. The rest of the sixth-formers were well into the sausages on beds of mashed potatoes.

The usual dinner table conversation flowed around Jay. The slightly-through-the-nose, upper-class English voices on either side of him and his father's all-American drawl leaping off the flimsy air-mail page in his pocket—*And I'd like to see Harvard try to turn you down with a record like*—

"I say, Fielding, if you haven't anything better to do this weekend, a few of us were thinking of taking the beagles out for a run. That is, of course, if the weather stays fine."

"What? Oh, I guess I can't make it. My mother and father are coming over." Jay put his hand inside his coat and touched the crinkly air mail envelope. Partly to quiet his father's voice. But his fingers touched the other envelope, the London one.

He drew it out and laid it in his lap. Etonian gentlemen don't read their letters at the table. He only
glanced down at the return address, Karen Beatty. He
looked at it blankly for a moment, not really seeing it.
Then, suddenly, he saw the three colors of a far-off
summer. The green of the hill, the flat blue water,
and the white house standing against white clouds.

8

Before London even began to stir on the gloomy Saturday morning, Karen was up and dressed. Two days since she'd sent the letter to Jay. Or had she only mailed a letter to a memory? He seemed as remote, as out-of-reach as . . . her own father. The letter was pointless. She hadn't even said anything in it, not anything she was feeling.

You don't write a short social note to a childhood friend and end it with *P.S. I think I am being held prisoner.* If there was a Jay, he was just another stranger in a world full of them, no one who could understand. Or help, if help was needed.

Still, she was sitting in the drawing-room chair nearest the hall. Calling herself names for never noticing exactly what time the mail was delivered. If Jay had received her letter, and if he'd written back the same day, today was the earliest possible time she might hear from him. Her only hope was to find the letter before anyone else did. Before Mrs. Plasket was up to brew the morning tea.

Karen felt eyes on her in the half-dark room. She scanned it to meet them. The big square blind eye of the television screen. Too dull to threaten. The twinkle of reflected light on the fireplace andirons—the only friendly glimmer in the room. Then she met the eyes in the picture on the piano. The little innocent child's eyes. Eleanor's.

She looked away, twisting around to check out the hall. Just in case the morning mail had slipped silently through the slot in the door. Nothing. Like the past two days. Nothing. And yet everything had changed. Blanche had dithered and bobbed along as usual. Syd had gone off to work and come home again. Mrs. Plasket had moved soundlessly through her routines.

But the difference was there. The house seemed like a stage set, *was* a stage set. Everything about it mocked her with its lifelessness. This was no family's home. She'd decided she could trust Mrs. Plasket that far at least. Nobody really lived there. Nobody Karen knew. Other tenants before, maybe. Other people, other strangers might have been living there last week. The kind of people who drift through furnished houses on the way to more furnished houses, keeping just ahead of—what—

And where were Syd and Blanche last week? And why were they here now? Questions. Karen couldn't chance asking any of them. If it were only a little bit longer, she thought. Only maybe today and tomorrow. I could handle that. But this could go on and on like a bad dream.

She must have slept. The room was brighter when she heard the sound. It brought her out of the chair like gunfire. The slap of mail hitting the hall floor and the retreating footsteps of the postman. They mingled with other footsteps before she could pull herself together.

Footsteps approaching from the kitchen end of the hall. As Karen moved for the doorway, Mrs. Plasket passed it, without seeing her. She stalked up to the mail and snatched it from the floor. As she turned, she saw Karen and blinked just once.

"Anything for me?" Karen asked, clearing her voice

at the same time. She had to say something. And she had to know. Mrs. Plasket looked surprised, just slightly. Then her face turned back to stone.

"Were you expecting something, miss?"

Karen wilted a little. She stepped back to keep from lunging at Mrs. Plasket. She had to know if there was something for her in that tight red fist.

"No. I . . . no, I just wondered. Shall I take them up to Mrs. Sutton?" Mrs Plasket's eyes stayed on her. Karen forced herself to meet the woman's gaze. Their eyes locked for a moment, and Mrs. Plasket broke first. She glanced down and fanned the two or three envelopes in her grip.

"Nothing much here this morning," she said calmly. "Circulars, from the look of them." Without turning away from Karen, she dropped the envelopes down on the little hall table.

"You'll be wanting your tea," she said and walked off down the hall.

Karen held herself in the drawing-room door as long as she could. Then she stepped across to the table and picked up the envelopes. They were brightly colored, with London postmarks. Advertisements, addressed to "Occupant." Junk mail. Karen's eyes blurred. Why had she let herself count so much on finding a letter that couldn't be there? Why count on a dim memory? Then she remembered that tomorrow would be Sunday. No mail delivery. Not even that to look forward to. Nothing.

She turned back toward the drawing room and almost stumbled. Only then the door at the kitchen end of the hall gently closed.

The morning crept by. Elevenses with Blanche, whose small talk seemed to be growing a little thin. Or was it Karen's imagination? She was listening to Blanche's chatter with new ears now, and yet it was

only more of the same. She yearned to ask Blanche
how long she and Syd had lived in the house. But she
kept her questions back. Better not to say anything to
reveal suspicion, or to create suspicion.

And yet she was determined to get to the bottom of
it all sooner or later. There'd already been too many
times in her life when she'd been expected to follow
blindly. She promised herself to find out this time,
whatever it cost her. Syd was home for the day by
lunch time, deep in a racing form he carried with him
to the table. Lunch was a pair of mealy Scotch eggs
with cream sauce, wrinkled peas and a sort of out-of-
seasonish salad. Karen found herself looking around
the blobs of food to the plate they were served on. A
smeary blue willow pattern of little oriental bridges
and drooping trees. Blanche dined off a plate covered
with pink and gray flowers, and Syd's was bone white
with a chipped gold band. Like a sort of high-level
rummage sale, Karen thought. If there was any conversation, she nodded through it.

She did hear mention of going out for tea, but that
was still hours away. Below table level, Karen pulled
the bottom button off her blazer and said she had
some mending to do.

Upstairs in her room, she replaced the button and
cross-stitched a gap in the lining. Where had she
learned to sew? She tried to remember if it was at
Dominion or the school before that. There didn't seem
to be enough memories to fill the time. By half past
two she was pacing the floor. I've got to be careful,
she thought, not to turn myself into a prisoner.

At three she was standing in the downstairs hall.
Blanche was napping in her room. Karen could hear
Mrs. Plasket moving around in the kitchen behind her.
There was so much of the house she hadn't seen.

The kitchen, of course, was Mrs. Plasket's territory
and off limits. And if these houses were like the brown-

stone ones in New York, there was a high basement where the kitchens used to be in the old days. What could be down there now? Dungeons, Karen thought and wondered for a second if she was actually trying to scare herself. And the steps out into the back courtyard. Albert's entrance.

Above her head, two, no, maybe three floors of bedrooms. The kind of place she had loved to explore when she was little. A ready-made Halloween house full of mysteries back when mysteries were fun. But not a house to explore now. Not with its creaking floorboards and unoiled hinges. She went into the drawing room, and Syd was sitting there.

A copy of *Sporting Life* was open on his lap. His head was thrown back in the chair. He was snoring lightly. He looked so harmless that Karen took a step forward, not really caring whether she woke him or not. Why is it that people look so different when they're asleep? More innocent. His tie hung loose from an open shirt collar. It was the old-fashioned detachable kind that fastened to the shirt with a little gold stud. He was a careless shaver and scruffy under the chin.

His conservative suitcoat gapped open, and Karen spotted a band of black leather. She couldn't take her eyes off it and wondered what it meant. Some weird fetish? Automatically, she took another step closer. The band ran down the side of his chest and would normally have been covered by his coat. It must have started in a loop over his shoulder. Then Karen knew. It was a shoulder holster. In a dark cavern of the rumpled coat she could see the handle of the revolver against Syd's white shirt.

Only then did she realize how near she was standing. She was practically hovering over him, and if he opened his eyes now . . .

A small part of her wanted to reach down and ease

the gun out. To hold in her hand simple Syd's sinister
toy. It was terrifying, of course. And certainly no toy,
yet satisfying in a peculiar way. It was evidence more
real than feelings and words. Evidence that everybody was playing a role. Syd was no tired London
businessman. In spite of his bowler hat that hung on
the hall tree, the neatly furled umbrella, the quiet suit.
No. London businessmen don't pack concealed weap-
ons. And if not a businessman, then what was he? And
who?

Karen moved back when she heard the sound outside. Someone had started up the front steps. The sudden noise crackled in the air. Surely it would bring
Syd out of a dead sleep. She walked backwards all the
way to the hall doorway and turned to see a shape in
silhouette through the front door's frosted glass pane.

Then she moved forward. Some instinct urged her
on to open that door before the caller knocked or located the bell. For some reason it was terribly important to open the door before the hand on the opposite
side reached out.

She was there in a second. In time. She struggled
with the lock and bolt arrangement, and on the other
side he could see that she was there. She knew he
wouldn't knock or ring. He'd wait, but she was hurry-
ing anyway, trying to ease the bolt back with a mini-
mum of noise. She glimpsed the shape beyond the
blurred glass. He was tall. It was too dark on the porch
to see if he was blond.

Then the door swung back toward her. Karen looked
up at him. He was blond.

"Oh, I hope you're Jay," she said without thinking,
almost without remembering to keep her voice down.

"Hello, Karen," Jay said.

9

"I thought the young gentlemen of Eton went around dressed like funeral directors," Karen said, eyeing Jay's nicely aged Levis and slightly tattered windbreaker.

They were on the top of a London bus, swaying down toward Chelsea. The door of the cage was open, and the bird flew, Karen thought. It all seemed miraculous. As unreal as everything that had happened, but now too good to be true.

She'd reached back for her coat and had pulled the door of 73A Cornwall Gardens firmly to behind her. And then they were walking off down the street, she and Jay. Four thousand miles and seven years from Lake Geneva, Wisconsin. He was a different Jay, of course. As tall and glorious as all the fictitious boys that boarding-school girls always pretend they know.

"You're either thinking of *Tom Brown's School Days* or *Goodbye, Mr. Chips*. Young gentlemen of Eton," Jay was saying, "manage to look as funky as possible the minute they get away from their tutors."

"I guess we're both a couple of escaped fugitives," Karen said, trying unsuccessfully to keep her tone light.

"Show a little respect," Jay said, lacing his fingers with hers. "I'm a privileged sixth-former with my A-level exams behind me now. So I rate all kinds of special deals, like Saturday afternoons in wicked old London. But about you I'm not so sure."

Karen was determined not to come on like a damsel in distress out of an old melodrama. For a few minutes she had let herself unwind. When they'd walked away from Cornwall Gardens, she hadn't even thought of looking back, much less going back. But of course she would go back. Before that, though, she'd have someone to tell her story to. Just getting it said would help. Getting it believed might be too much to hope for.

"It was a hard letter to write, Jay. It would have been hard even if I'd been surer it would get to you."

On top of the bus. . . . in a long walk down the Saturday carnival of the King's Road . . . in a dizzy steel and plastic "juice bar". . . in all these improbable settings, Karen told Jay the story of the most recent week of her life.

It was odd, taking every event in order, dissecting these few days, when there were years between them and the children they'd been at Lake Geneva. How different from those letters she used to write to a Jay who never read them. He listened quietly, taking it all in without interruption.

The story grew filmy in Karen's mind at some points. She tried to stick to the facts. The trench-coat man at Shannon. Mrs. Plasket. Syd's gun. They were easy enough to describe. But other things: waiting for word from Dad, the feeling she had when she looked at the picture of Eleanor, the weird, half-normal atmosphere of the Suttons' house; these were harder to put into words.

Things she could only sense or wonder about merged into imagination. Imagination led straight to spaced-out hysteria. She tried to tell it all calmly. What was it Miss Sands, her English teacher, always advised? In telling a story, keep your audience in mind. Don't get carried away.

As she came to the end, the thought of having to go back to Cornwall Gardens descended on her. There the two of them sat at a glass table in a bustling Chelsea hangout called The Tantalized Tulip drinking room-temperature orangeade to the background thump of acid rock.

"Well, that's the story," Karen said, tracing a thin line of spilled orange liquid across the table. "At least as much of it as I know. There's more, of course. More about . . . my father." She hesitated, looked up at Jay's eyes, trying to read them. "'My father . . . I haven't seen very much of him for a long time. I used to try to say to myself that he was like anybody's father. But—"

"What are you trying to say, Karen?"

"That he's mixed up in some kind of crime syndicate, that something's happened to him because of that. That the Suttons—"

"Could be either friend or foe and you don't know which?" Jay finished the question.

"Yes."

"Well then, you can't take any chances with them. And besides you've left something out."

"Believe me, I know. It's a story full of loose ends."

"No," Jay said, "I mean something specific. I don't think you noticed it," he said. "But when you opened the door this afternoon, there was someone standing behind you, back by the stairs."

"Mrs. Plasket," Karen half whispered.

"No. I don't know what Mrs. Plasket looks like, but you can be sure she wasn't standing there. It was a guy. A young guy."

"Albert," Karen said.

* * *

They walked back up Gloucester Road from Chelsea, letting the buses pass them by in fuming red lines. They'd been away more than an hour. Even though Karen dreaded going back, she was curious. Curious to know how Blanche and Syd would react. She remembered that first morning when she'd innocently strolled out of the house. It seemed years ago, yet she was bringing it back. Remembering the look on Blanche's face when she'd come in.

"I don't know what's going on, Karen. But I don't want you going back there." They were walking arm and arm, and Jay was staring ahead. It was so good to have an ally that Karen was almost happy for those moments. "Besides, now that I've found you again—or you've found me or whatever—I hate to give you up."

"It doesn't matter to you that my father's a—"

"It doesn't matter to me if he's King of the Godfathers. It's you I'm thinking about."

They paced on in silence for a few feet. "But I have to go back, don't I?" Karen said. "Unless you can smuggle me into Eton as an overlooked first-year boy."

The idea was Shakespearean, but un-Etonian. Karen with her softly spectacular figure as a stand-in for weedy Desmond Hoaresham-D'ark was too rich a thought to pass over lightly. But Jay was too concerned with the problem at hand.

"Look, my folks are getting here tomorrow. I can take you down to the Doncaster today, right now. You can check in, and then tomorrow we can ask them what we ought to do." Jay slipped his arm around her shoulders and pulled her close. He was so satisfied with his new idea that he seemed poised and ready to sweep her onto the next bus heading for Doncaster.

"No," Karen said, half smiling at him and shaking her head.

"But why not? Why take a chance? You know something funny's going on and you've convinced me. I don't want you to go back. Tomorrow—"

"No. Jay. I know what you're saying. But I've got to go back there."

"Why? If you don't, they're obviously not going to call the police and report you missing. They wouldn't risk it."

"Wouldn't they? How do we know what they'd risk when we don't know who they are?"

"If you don't go back, it won't matter what they do. Tomorrow—"

"Tomorrow your parents will get here. But they're your parents, Jay, not mine. They won't even remember me."

"That won't matter to them. They—"

"They haven't got the solution, Jay. Parents hardly ever do. I've been on my own long enough to know that."

"Now wait a minute, Karen. I've been over *here* in school for five years. I know what being away from home's like."

"Yes, but you've always had a home to go back to. I haven't. But we're off the track. There's another reason I have to go back. There's some kind of link between the Suttons and my father."

"But you don't think your father's going to contact you there, do you?"

It was the question she hadn't faced up to on her own. She could feel herself wavering, responding to the pressure of Jay's arm around her shoulder.

"No. I don't think he's going to contact me there or turn up or . . ." She didn't trust her voice, and swallowed hard.

"Then you can't go on faking it with them, and there's no point. Besides, when they see me, they'll know."

"When they see you, it ought to be interesting," she

said, pulling herself back together. "Anyway, they must already know about you. Albert probably told them." She glanced over her shoulder at the crowded pavement behind them, but it was a mass of strangers. "It's probably a good thing if they realize I know someone else in London. You're my secret weapon."

Jay wasn't ready to give up. He tried another angle. "This Miss Simon you told me about, your father's secretary. You could come to the hotel and send a cable to her. Or call her."

Karen was silent, waiting for Jay to think it through. It seemed to be Miss Simon who'd masterminded everything. And even if she hadn't, even if somebody had been working from her office . . . "I have to go back, Jay. I'm tired of being lied to and manipulated. I've made a little deal with myself about that. I've got to find out just what the Suttons are trying to do."

"You're stubborn, aren't you?"

"Maybe."

"You've found out enough already, maybe too much."

"Suspecting isn't knowing. I've got to—"

"It's your mother, isn't it? It's not being sure whether they're her relatives. That's what's eating you, isn't it?"

"Yes," Karen said, and realized it for the first time.

They'd turned off Gloucester Road, and the trees in the Cornwall Gardens square lay ahead of them.

"Karen, while there's still time—"

"While there's still time, I'll make a deal with you," she said. "I'll go back now, but I'll meet you tomorrow, you and your parents at the Doncaster. If I'm not there by noon—"

"No," Jay broke in. "It's too risky. If you're going back there, I'm going to spend the night on the front steps. I'm not leaving you."

"Jay, somehow the thought of you on the front steps overnight just doesn't reassure me like it should. Now will you listen? I'll meet you and your parents at the Doncaster tomorrow. And if I'm not there at noon, you can come here and find out why."

"Somehow that doesn't reassure *me* like it should," Jay said, throwing her words back at her.

"But you understand why I want to do it this way, don't you?"

"I guess so. Part of it anyway. But I certainly don't understand all of it."

"Neither do I." They were standing at the bottom of the steps of 73A. Karen tried to keep herself from looking up at the windows of the house. But she couldn't keep from it. They were blank. No curtain twitched. They walked up the steps together. Jay's arm still firm around her shoulders. The door was unlatched, open a fraction of an inch.

Karen remembered having pulled it shut behind her when she'd left. She pushed the door open into an empty hall. Could they be gone? She started in, trying to slip away from Jay's arm, but he stayed with her. They stood silent for a moment. There was the sound of Mrs. Plasket rattling pans in the kitchen. Karen stepped up to the drawing-room doorway. Syd's arm was draped over the chair arm, and his feet sprawled across the carpet. They could both hear the steady bubbling murmur of his half-snore.

Karen turned and gave Jay a gentle nudge toward the door. He was managing to look both suspicious and bewildered. "All quiet," she whispered to him. "Now go. I'll see you tomorrow." She turned to start up the stairs, but he stood rooted to the spot. She stepped back to him and started to give him another nudge in the direction of the door, but he took hold of her arms and drew her close. Her head slipped into the hollow of his shoulder as he bent to kiss her. For a half minute Karen forgot everything. Then she pushed him out the door.

"Tomorrow," he said, forgetting to whisper, "at the Doncaster."

It was all a little too easy, she thought once she'd made it up to her room. Getting back in undiscovered. It must have been staged, like everything else. She could sense it. It was funny how sharp the senses could be once they were needed. The front door so conveniently left off the latch. By Mrs. Plasket? Syd convincingly asleep. No Albert lurking around in the shadows. But what next?

She couldn't help feeling defensive, as if the next move wasn't hers. She looked at the bedroom door she'd just closed behind her. Any minute now, she thought, Blanche will burst through that door and demand to know where I've been and who Jay is. We'll all be out in the open then.

Karen was so convinced that she stood listening for the approaching tap of Blanche's high heels. But there was nothing. Staring at the door gave her another idea worse than a raging Blanche. They could lock her in. That was the one thing she couldn't face. She darted for the door to try it in case a hand had turned a silent key in the lock on the hallway side.

The door opened easily. She examined the catch. It was half rusted out. No one had locked that door in decades. She eased it shut again and turned back to the room. Mustn't panic, she told herself. Nothing to get panicky over. Now that Jay knew, everything would work out.

She tried to tranquilize herself by remembering how hopeless she'd felt only a few hours before when there was no letter in the mail. Tomorrow she would see Jay. But now that she was back, Jay was as remote as before. And tomorrow was as far off as yesterday.

Karen decided that it was being alone that was getting her down. Being alone after being with Jay. She walked around the screen to bathe her eyes in cold water and caught a glimpse of herself in the wavery old mirror above the sink. Of course, Karen said very slowly to herself, I could be losing my mind.

There was a quick little knock at the koor. Like a bird pecking. And Blanche walked in.

"My dear, I must have overslept! What a bore! When I'd thought we might run up to Derry and Tom's roof garden for tea. What a tiresome afternoon for you and what an awful hostess I am!" She delivered her little speech beautifully, Karen thought.

Blanche was in a well-worn wrapper, a silk print of palm trees and hibiscus blossoms. Her hair was a post-nap rat's nest, but her sharp little bird's eyes glittered as if she hadn't slept in a week. They decided on an at-home tea, and Blanche vanished to "put on something decent."

The hours between tea time and midnight stretched endlessly. The play-acting went ahead as usual. No hint of suspicion, no menacing undertone. Just Blanche's endless stories about "poor, dear Eleanor" and the old days. An Eleanor that Karen no longer believed in. They're keeping me from my real father and offering me a fake mother instead, she thought. But she sat quietly through the hours, trying to keep the scream back, a scream more of frustration than of fear.

Only the thought of tomorrow, of getting away from this subtle, sociable prison kept her steady. It had been so easy to walk out that afternoon. Would it be that easy again? Surely they knew she'd been out. Surely they couldn't let that happen again. But the thought of waiting until tomorrow alone in her bedroom kept her downstairs in the drawing room as long

as possible. Finally, Syd was fast asleep in his chair
again and even Blanche was covering yawns.

Then she was in her room, standing against the
closed door, listening as Blanche and Syd passed by
on the way to their room at the back. Mrs. Plasket had
turned down Karen's bed. She'd obviously finished up
her chores long since. It was strange, but Karen would
almost have welcomed the sight of her, of almost anyone.

As she undressed for bed, she tried to plan for tomorrow, but could get no farther than remembering
she'd need money if she could get away. Money and
the passport. Extra clothes were out of the question.
She walked over and pulled out the bottom drawer
where she'd left the folder with the money and passport.

She'd left it under a stack of underwear. Her hand
didn't find it, and she lifted out the clothes. The
drawer was empty. She reached up to the next one,
but before she pulled it open, she knew it was useless.
A moment later she was standing in front of the four
gaping drawers of the old chest. The four empty
drawers.

Her only thought was that she couldn't stay in the
room another minute. She could almost visualize Mrs.
Plasket's large red hands as they must have explored
the drawers.

She pulled on her robe and walked to the door, put
her ear against it for a moment, and then stepped out
into the black hall. There were unexplored doors all
along it, and at the end a streak of light under the
door to Blanche and Syd's room.

Karen stood there, with no place to go. The thought
of Albert possibly somewhere in the dark house almost sent her back to her room. But the light under
the far door drew her on. She took one step at a time

on freezing feet. There were little unexpected throw rugs, but most of the floor was bare and as cold as a tombstone.

They were talking, though Karen's nose almost touched their door before she could hear the words. Blanche's voice was low, but it had a cutting edge. "The stupid clods! They might have killed him and then where would we be? The stupid, idiotic animals!"

Syd's voice seemed to be muffled by bed clothes, ". . . hired to give him a proper scare, and that's what they did."

"Yes, a proper scare, you may well say! He's been in a coma the better part of a week from all accounts, and what good does that do us, I'd like to know? And just how long are we to—"

Karen stepped back, turned and ran over the skittering rugs. She was in her room, suddenly a safe haven. Her heart roared, and she fell into the bed, twisted in her robe. She knew who it was, who it had to be. She knew they were talking about her father.

After a while she dreamed, though she would have sworn she was awake. A hospital ward, a long corridor of dirty white, nearly familiar. And a woman in a long robe printed with palm trees and hibiscus blossoms leaning over a bed.

Karen dream-walked through the corridor trying to draw closer to the woman who wavered at first far away and then suddenly near. It was Blanche, of course, but Karen was straining to see the bed she hovered over. A hospital bed with levers and pulleys, all white and chipped paint.

And on it a figure wrapped like a mummy. In the soundless dream Karen saw the flash of metal in Blanche's hand. The scissors with blades that opened and closed like a bird's bill as Blanche cut through the bandages that shaped to form a man's body. The scissors' blades gnawed at the wrapping, but the figure's head was a smooth dome of featureless plaster.

Karen knew whose face would be behind that egg-shaped white mask.

"Dad—" Like all nightmares the will to scream was stifled. A cold hand across her mouth sealed the sound of screaming inside her. A hand heavy enough to pin her head against the pillow.

The light blinded her, but the hand remained. Something brushed the side of Karen's face, something nightmarish but absolutely real. She was awake and squinting to see. It was a gray pigtail, swaying near her neck. The hand loosened its grip on her mouth. She could see Mrs. Plasket's face, inches from her own. Bending over her just as Blanche in the dream had bent over.

"Quietly now, miss," Mrs. Plasket whispered. "You didn't ought to make a sound. Get up and dress yourself." Mrs. Plasket's mop of hair was pulled into two pigtails, and she wore a man's tattered bathrobe. Her middle-of-the-night face was a mass of loose folds, too soft to be stony.

Karen slipped out of bed like an obedient child. She could only feel relief at being rescued from the nightmare. She was half dressed before she realized how well she was taking orders from this woman. Mrs. Plasket stood directly behind her. When Karen turned, buttoning up the coat of her tweed suit, she saw that Mrs. Plasket's eyes were trained on the door. I don't have any choice, Karen thought. I'll have to do what she wants.

Mrs. Plasket reached past her into the wardrobe and pulled Karen's heavy coat out—gently to keep the hanger from rattling. "Carry your shoes," she whispered, and nodded toward the door.

Like leaving the airplane, Karen thought, her mind whirling. The hall was as black as before, with the same strip of light below the door at the end of it. Karen turned toward the front of the house. But Mrs. Plasket's hand fell on her shoulder, drawing her back the other way. They moved silently toward the door to Blanche and Syd's room. She's taking me to them, Karen thought, wanting to break and run. But she knew it was hopeless. Mrs. Plasket seemed to surround her on all sides like an enormous shadow.

They were near enough to hear the muted mumble of voices. Karen heard Blanche's voice die away suddenly. Then, "Listen, did you hear that?"

"Hear what?" Syd's voice replied.

Mrs. Plasket froze and clamped Karen's shoulder tighter. Karen stood immobile, waiting for the door in front of her to fly open. But Mrs. Plasket was drawing her to one side, through another door. It seemed to be a closet. The old woman's hand slipped down along Karen's arm, finding her wrist. And then they were edging sideways down a flight of twisting, invisible stairs. One careful step as a time.

At the bottom they seemed to be in the kitchen. Karen felt the clammy cold of a tile floor beneath her feet. Mrs. Plasket moved behind her, closed a door behind them both, and eased a bolt across it. They stood there a moment, the two of them, both listening for sounds above. But there was nothing. Karen only heard her own breathing.

At last Mrs. Plasket stepped closer and whispered directly into her ear, "You must go now—get right away from this house."

Karen stood unmoving.

"That young lad you went out with yesterday. Can you go to him?" Karen nodded, and the old woman was near enough to understand.

"Then go, and don't let them near you again, any of them."

"My father—"

"While they have you, they have a hold on your father. Without you, they—"

"Who are you, Mrs. Plasket?"

"I'm nothing to do with them. But I knew they weren't right the minute I came to work here. Didn't they create when they found you gone yesterday. Nearly off their heads they were!"

The house creaked. And was silent again. "Low class is what they are. You can hear it in their speech. They're no better than—"

Another creak. The sound of dry leaves swirling out in the courtyard. "Get right away, miss. Lose you, and they've failed in their—"

"Where's Albert?"

"Downstairs where he sleeps. We'll have to pass his door, but never mind. He only does as he's told. And he's dull enough wide awake."

They crossed the kitchen. A glow of pale light from a high window outlined the dark round shapes of pans hanging along the walls. There was another flight of stairs, straight, but narrow, that led down to the cellar. Mrs. Plasket moved ahead, drawing Karen on with one hand. She walked faster, sure of her footing, and they were in another dark hallway, heading toward the front of the house. Passing by the room where Albert slept.

The door ahead of them was off the latch. Mrs. Plasket only had to swing it open. She eased Karen past her. As she stepped through the door, Karen felt the fresh outdoor air. She was standing in a covered space directly below the little front porch. There was a row of "dust bins" in the narrow well between the front of the house and steps that led up to street level. The tradesman's entrance. Mrs. Plasket's territory.

Karen turned back to her, and Mrs. Plasket handed over her heavy winter coat.

"Why?"

"It's nothing to do with me," Mrs. Plasket said. "Be off." The door closed between them.

Karen stood there a moment, still in the shadows. Then she slipped on her shoes and started up the steps, carefully bypassing the metal cans. The south street of Cornwall Gardens stretched into the morning mist in both directions. Karen turned to walk toward Gloucester Road, the only way she knew. But the emptiness of the early Sunday morning pavements was terrifying. She could imagine herself a few paces farther on with the sudden sound of running footsteps behind her.

She turned the other way, but it was a long, stark row of houses leading into the unknown. She crossed the street then, into the neat, manicured grove of trees in the midst of Cornwall Gardens square.

It was like a miniature forest, but too sparse for cover. Karen felt the windows of the house behind her boring into her back like eyes as she walked in the spongy grass. An identical wall of houses faced her on the opposite side. Rows of cars lined both streets, but they were parked. Nothing moved.

It was getting lighter. The wet morning air caught in her lungs. She leaned against a tree trunk for a moment, hoping it concealed her from behind. She scanned the other street in the square, hoping to find a little opening she could make a run for. There seemed to be one small alleyway.

Then behind her she heard a sudden noise. The rattle and bang of a door being unbolted. She pulled the skirt of her long winter coat around her, and tried to become a part of the narrow tree. Footsteps scraped on the porch of 73A. She knew without looking that they had burst out onto the porch and were looking up and down the street.

"Get Albert! Ring up the others!" she heard Blanche's voice echo across the square. "And keep your voice down!" But only Blanche's voice was audible.

A century passed. Then Karen heard the rushing footsteps. They struck the sidewalk at a running pace. She held her breath, grateful that they weren't heading across the street and up behind her. Far off down the street, she heard a car motor grind into life. Then roar into action. By turning her head slightly, she could see it in the distance, U-turning and heading down toward Gloucester Road. But they weren't all in the car, she thought. Perhaps only Syd or Albert.

She stood there, feeling the bark of the tree against the back of her head. Her hair was matted and tangled in the roughness of the tree. She plunged her hands farther down into her coat pockets, still holding its folds close around her legs.

Then her numb hand felt something in one of the pockets. A flat folder. She explored it with her fingers and knew what it was without drawing it out. The folder with her money and the passport, where Mrs. Plasket must have put it for safekeeping.

10

Even at midmorning, the dining room of the Doncaster Hotel was almost empty. Most of the waiters stood as solemn as penguins beside the glittering silver covers of the breakfast buffet.

"It's no use," the woman with the well-waved gray hair and the pearls shook her head. "I can't *possibly* drink this coffee. We should be sticking to tea."

"Mother," Jay said, "let's get back to—"

"Now, honey, we've been over it. Your father and I are simply exhausted from that flight. My feet still hurt from pounding those New York sidewalks, and I don't even *remember* when I slept last."

"It beats the devil out of me how you got hooked up with this Beatty girl after all these years anyway." Mr. Fielding's voice was a hoarse, morning growl. "Why, I don't even know how you could remember her. And now *this*," he slapped the folded newspaper lying next to his plate. "It's all over the New York papers."

"Now, Sam," Mrs. Fielding said, "we haven't seen Jay in nearly a year, and we have so many plans to make for him. Don't spoil—"

"I'm not about to spoil anything for anybody. But I'm not having our boy mixed up in anything like this . . . this bunch of underworld characters."

"Dad, look." Jay twisted the heavy napkin on his lap into a rigid knot. "When Karen told me what was hap-

pening to her, I didn't know what to think. Now there's
the proof that she needs us to help her." Jay looked at
the newspaper. "It's not her fault, Dad. But she's in
trouble."

"People like us don't get involved in trouble like—"

Jay looked up. Across the room at the entrance
flanked by great sprays of spring flowers Karen was
standing.

Her coat was over her arm, and she wore a well-
tailored tweed suit. Her long hair lay smoothly over
her shoulders. She looked more like a well-heeled
young tourist than an escaped prisoner. Jay pushed
his chair back and walked quickly toward her, away
from his father's voice.

He put out his arms to her, well aware of his parents' eyes behind him. "You made it."

"With a little help from my friends," Karen replied,
looking up with the small half-smile she'd already
adopted for Jay.

"I'd like to know who your friends are," Jay said,
"your other friends, I mean."

"Well, Mrs. Plasket, as it turned out. Then later, the
ladies' room attendant here at the hotel. She let me
lurk in her lair for hours, and I managed to pull myself
together."

"Thank God you're all right." Jay touched her gently on the cheek. "Come and meet my folks," he said
and groaned a little without meaning to.

Mr. Fielding rose reluctantly out of his chair when
Jay led Karen up to the table. The waiter slid a chair
smoothly in behind her. "Why, this must be Karen,"
Mrs. Fielding said in a voice that bounced around the
room. "The last time I saw you, you were just a cute
little thing, and now—"

"Margaret, will you cut the cocktail-party chatter?
Do you realize the police are out looking for this girl?"

Mr. Fielding's growl cut across his wife's voice. He turned on Karen, "What is all this about your father?"

"I don't know," she said quietly. "I just don't—"

"You mean you don't know about this?" Mr. Fielding thrust the newspaper at her. It was a New York paper, folded open to an article with a blaring black headline.

"Dad, please," Jay said, but Karen reached for the paper.

CRIME FIGURE FIRE VICTIM REMAINS CRITICAL
WOMAN EMPLOYEE FOUND
DAUGHTER STILL MISSING

Stephen Beatty, 48, New York businessman and alleged underworld leader, continues to fight for his life in a local hospital. Police refuse to identify his present whereabouts, but he is known to be under heavy protective guard.

Sources report that Beatty, whose business ventures are a reputed front for big-time criminal activities, is still on the critical list after a spectacular attempt on his life.

The drama began late Sunday night as Beatty returned to his East Side apartment. Unknown assailants jumped from a car, doused him with gasoline, and set him afire before the stunned gaze of the doorman. The attackers escaped, apparently without a trace. Beatty was rushed to a hospital suffering from severe burns.

Police remain baffled by the attack, but underworld sources call it the work of a rival worldwide syndicate. New York has been rocked in recent months by increased inter-gang warfare.

The alleged crime leader's enemies are steadily

moving in on the choice territory of the Beatty
empire. The attack is thought to be a forceful
threat rather than a murder attempt.

A usually reliable informer is quoted as saying,
"With his connections, Beatty's worth more to
them alive than dead. They'll lean on him all they
can."

Karen's mind fought the reality of the words on the
page. She forced herself to read on:

DAUGHTER VANISHES

Police investigating Beatty's East 57th Street
business office Monday found it ransacked and
deserted. His secretary, Jeanette Simon, about 30,
spent Monday at the bedside of her employer,
but later eluded authorities as she left the hospital and was not located until yesterday. She was
found in a Margate, New Jersey, hotel, registered
under an assumed name.

Held for questioning, Ms. Simon revealed that
she received an anonymous telephone message at
the hospital late Monday afternoon. The unidenti-
fied caller told her that Beatty's daughter, Karen,
16, had been lured away from her fashionable
Connecticut boarding school and would be held
until her father was able "to agree to terms" with
her abductors. The caller warned Ms. Simon to
do nothing until she was next contacted.

To check the story, Ms. Simon explained that
she had called Karen Beatty's school. She learned
from the headmistress that a woman claiming to
be Ms. Simon herself had instructed that the
Beatty girl be sent to New York with her passport.

Surmising that the girl was to be taken out of

the country, Ms. Simon checked all foreign flights. She was able to ascertain that a Karen Beatty was booked aboard a BOAC flight to London. Too late to stop the plane and reluctant to involve the police, Ms. Simon admitted to calling in a false bomb threat which grounded the plane early Tuesday morning at Shannon Airport. Ms. Simon contacted a man in Ireland who she would identify only as an "Irish member of Mr. Beatty's business organization" to rescue Karen Beatty.

He failed in the attempt, and the girl continued to London. She is known to have passed through customs at London Airport, but her present whereabouts . . .

Karen read through the story of the past week in her life, gripping the edges of the newspaper. Her eyes kept returning to the early paragraphs: "Unknown assailants jumped from a car, soused him with gasoline, and set him afire. . . ." She couldn't absorb it all.

It answered questions, some of them. It began to explain Judy, that slick little actress. And the man in the trench coat at Shannon, who was only trying to keep her from the Suttons. But it didn't answer everything. It didn't tell her if her father was dead or alive. It only verified what she'd always known he was, leaving her no way to deny it any more.

"Well, if you didn't know, you know now," Mr. Fielding said. His words were harsh, but there was a half-apologetic sound in his voice. "Now don't tell us you didn't know your father's a—"

"Dad, leave Karen alone!"

She looked at Mr. Fielding. "Yes, I guess I always knew," she said quietly.

"Karen," Jay said, reaching over to cover her hand with his, "what do you want to do now?"

Mr. Fielding cleared his voice noisily in the background.

"I want to go home to be with him. I want to go home right now."

"Of course you do, dear," Mrs. Fielding said. She bobbed her head in Karen's direction, reminding her suddenly of Blanche. She shuddered and felt the urge to look quickly behind her, across the snowy white tablecloths of the elegant dining room.

"Come on," Jay said. "We'll take you out to the airport right now and get you on a plane to New York."

He was half out of his chair when his father said, "Not so fast, if all this wild stuff we've been hearing is true. Karen's got some obligations right here. I think we'd better give the American Embassy a call. I have a friend in the diplomatic corps who might be able—"

"Dad, this isn't the time to tell us about what good connections you've got." Mr. Fielding's eyes flared at his son, but Jay stared him down.

"We'll notify the British police from the airport. And the sooner we can get out there the better," Jay said.

"You don't think she's in any danger here, do you?" Mrs. Fielding was aghast. "Why this is *England!*"

Karen and Jay walked out of the dining room, too fast for his parents to keep up with them. Mrs. Fielding fluttered and struggled with her mink. Mr. Fielding fumed and had to be pursued by the waiter who wanted him to sign for the breakfasts.

The walk to the portico where the cabs drew up to the Doncaster lay across a grand lobby. Bellboys in bandbox hats crisscrossed the deep carpet. More spring flowers stood in silver vases beside the revolving door.

Just before they stepped into the door, Jay stopped and said, "Karen, I'm sorry . . . about my folks."

"It's all right," she said. "All I want now is to be with my father."

"I wish I were going with you."

Something made Karen look past Jay just then. There were tears welling up in her eyes, but she blinked them away. A car had drawn up under the portico beyond the revolving door. Two men got out. One was a stranger—like an enormous gorilla. The other one was Syd.

Karen reached for Jay's arm and turned her head away. Had Syd seen her? A moment later and they'd have been entangled in the revolving door—all four of them.

She pulled Jay into a little alcove behind one of the sprays of spring flowers. The two men never looked in their direction. They walked quickly across the lobby past an astonished Mrs. Fielding.

Karen and Jay were in the revolving doors a second later.

"Is that their car?" Jay muttered as they passed the doorman.

Karen nodded, knowing what they were about to do. They parted to enter the car from opposite sides, each managing to move slowly enough to attract no attention. The motor was still running.

Jay slipped the car into gear and swung it out into the open lane of the drive. Karen looked back to see the revolving door move. Mr. and Mrs. Fielding stumbled out of it. They stared after the retreating car, their mouths frozen in amazed, gaping circles.

Jay eased the car expertly down one street and up another and once through a sleepy mews only a lane wide. He didn't settle to a respectable speed until they emerged in Berkeley Square. They cruised around two sides of it, past the morning dog-walkers, and shot down Berkeley Street in the direction of Piccadilly.

"This isn't solving anything, is it?" Karen said, set-

tling back for the first time as Jay continued to lose
them in London.

"What do you mean?"

"I mean you can't take me to the airport. They'll
have it staked out, as the saying goes. They want me
back, and we don't know how many of them there
are."

"A lot, I guess," Jay said, never taking his eyes off
the street ahead. "Back at the hotel, how did you
know—"

"One of them was Syd. He must have heard you
mention the Doncaster yesterday. I don't know who
the other one was. I suppose that was a break. I might
have been grabbed by somebody I didn't know. I
nearly didn't recognize Syd until it was too late."

Jay executed another turn just ahead of a changing
traffic light. "I don't want to go to the police," Karen
said, reading his mind. "I'm afraid they'll hold me
here—in protective custody or whatever—while they
try to round up the Suttons and the rest of them,
whoever it was that put the Suttons up to it. Come to
think of it, I suppose the police will be keeping an eye
on the airport too, especially if they know I've gotten
away. And your parents will tell them that. They'll be
frantic."

"I suppose so," Jay said. "My father'll be mad, and
my mother's probably bewildered. I guess that adds
up to frantic. But the point is, it looks like I'm stuck
with the most wanted woman in Europe." He looked
at Karen, trying to coax a smile out of her. They drove
halfway across London before she spoke again.

"A long time ago, I went to school with a girl named
Bea Callaghan. She said we were two of a kind because our fathers were both in the same kind of business. See? I can't even quite say it yet. Anyway, Bea
was the kind of girl who adusted to it, her background, I mean. But I didn't. It was easier to pretend.

And now look at the mess I'm in, and you with me. I guess everything catches up with you sooner or later, all the little lies. I suppose it's time I started thinking like a criminal's daughter."

"What does that mean?"

"I don't know. It's too new. Maybe it means the world's full of all kinds of hard facts they don't teach you to face in boarding school. Maybe it even means that the policeman you're always taught is your best friend isn't my best friend. It might even mean I'm not entitled to the kind of protection other people have."

"You're still yourself, Karen."

"How can I be when I've never begun to know who I am until now?"

"Well, you'll have me for company in your identity crisis."

"It's my crisis," Karen said. "It's not going to be over even when I can get home. And it's not fair to you— you've got to get back to your family and to Eton."

"You're not the only escapee, Karen. I've got reasons of my own. My family and my future, I need to get away from all that myself for a while."

They were barreling down a wide highway, leaving London behind. "How far do you think we can get in a hot car?" Karen asked.

"No telling, considering we stole it from crooks. You don't think they'd forget who they are and report it to Scotland Yard, do you?"

Karen tried to feel relief in the nearness of Jay and the distance from the Suttons. It was a relief, and yet the whole world was still a prison, as if she and Jay would drive to wherever this road ended only to find a high stone wall, penning them in with enemies she didn't even know.

"Who do suppose they were?" J asked, entering her thoughts. "The Suttons, I mean."

"Part of a plan," Karen said. "People playing a role,

doing as they were told. Now that I think about it, I don't even know if they were married to each other. They were pretty good too, up to a point. I suppose it was smarter of them to keep me fooled than to keep me locked up. Safer too. It would have seened so ordinary to anybody who might have been watching.

"But I should have known. It was all so sudden and new. But still, I should have known."

"Forget them."

"I wish I could. Maybe I will when I'm sure, when I'm out of England. ow I hate them for using my mother. All Blanche's talk about Eleanor. I always wanted to know about my mother, and then suddenly I was hearing about her. And the picture of the little girl. It could've been any little girl. It could even have been Blanche." Karen felt suddenly sick. "Where are we going?"

"Someplace where we can catch our breath, a long way from the Doncaster and Cornwall Gardens. The only safe place I can think of."

11

The big stucco house rose like a rock along the steep hill. Its dormers looked out across the curving line of Saunton Sands far below. The shallow sea sent waves in long, phosphorescent patterns onto the beach.

The windows on the sea side were lit only by reflected moonlight. Above the house the coast road twisted around the headland and on to the deserted resort towns of Croyde and Woolacombe and Mortehoe.

It was late when Karen and Jay drove up the headland road to the home of the Hoaresham-D'arks. Halfway along from London, Jay had pulled off at a roadside pub outside Salisbury. He'd made a call to Wykeham House and had miraculously got through to Desmond, who was spending a monotonous Sunday afternoon staring at a Latin grammar, he said.

Desmond had been intrigued and then overjoyed to offer to Jay his parents' house down in Devon. He pledged himself to undying secrecy against any questions that might come from the Fieldings or the house tutor. Jay had returned to the pub's parking lot with a head full of plans and a handful of meat pies and bottled cider.

Following Desmond's breathless directions, Jay located the entrance to the drive that dipped sharply down from the main road to the big house. It was only a gap in the rhododendron hedge, ending in a circle of gravel before the front door.

They had discussed abandoning the car, but rejected the idea. They might need it. There was a garage built into a wing of the house, but Jay could see the Hoaresham-D'ark Rolls Royce through a window in the door. They had left it behind when they went to Madeira.

Jay killed the motor and cut the lights. The car was screened from the road. And the tiny space between hillside and house seemed the darkest place in England. So silent they could hear the singing of the sea.

"Scared?" Jay asked, finding Karen's hand.

"Of the dark or of you?"

"Well, after all those years of being locked up in the best schools, here we are alone together, like the old songs say. Anything could happen."

"Somehow I have the feeling everything that could ever happen already has."

When they got out of the car, the house towering over them sent a shiver through Karen. She'd be a long time getting over that other house in Cornwall Gardens, maybe forever.

The key was under the mat, as Desmond said it would be. They stepped like thieves past an umbrella stand and into the big, open entrance hall. Through glass doors they could see into a large room paved in light that fell through the long windows.

Jay walked ahead and opened the doors into what was probably a luxurious sitting room. It was furnished with the glimmer of silver and the geometric shapes of moonlight. Beyond, a terrace over the sea glowed like rock salt. But Karen stood her ground in the darker entry hall. She glanced to one side.

A stairway rose to a landing with a window. Framed in the window someone was standing, a fig-

of her dusty-rose dressing gown fanning out behind her.

They had their coffee in front of an electric fire at the end of the big room that Mrs. Hoaresham called "the lounge." The moon was long gone, and the orange bars in the grate bathed the two young faces and the old one in a warm glow.

"How very like Desmond to forget about me entirely in his zeal to offer you this house!" Mrs. Hoaresham explained. "I do hope he has remembered my existence since and is writhing in suspense!"

"I believe he thought you had gone to Monte Carlo, Mrs. Hoaresham," Jay said, trying not to grin.

"I leave day after tomorrow. Except for the war years, I have gone to Monte Carlo every spring since 1933. Desmond's parents have been in Madeira a week. I enjoy having the house to myself as much as going on holiday. And," she added, "it is particularly providential that I stayed behind this year."

Mrs. Hoaresham's mind seemed to take quick turns as she explored the situation from all angles. It was clearer by the minute that she enjoyed the sudden involvement with these two young foreigners.

"No, I think on the whole that we won't call in the police in this matter. They will, as you say, Karen, delay the proceedings interminably. Such a lot of red tape. No, our problem is to get you home to your father as quickly as we can. Your father's enemies are obviously an impressive conspiracy. We three can conspire as well."

She rose then. "And now we need some rest. We are liable to need it. Tomorrow we will take steps. I have a feeling that we have every reason for making haste."

Mrs. Hoaresham looked down at Karen then. "You are being very brave, my dear. You will need all your bravery when you are home again.

"And now to bed. There is a couch in my dressing
room for you, Karen. And you, young man, will oc-
cupy Desmond's room at the far end of the hall."

Karen and Jay trailed Mrs. Hoaresham up the stairs,
like two well-behaved very sleepy children.

Karen awoke, grateful for a dreamless night. Almost
dreamless. Just as she was waking, she caught a
glimpse of her father. He reached out to her. But then
he was gone.

Getting out of bed, she tripped over the hem of the
billowing nightgown that hung on her. It belonged to
Desmond's mother, a fine wool one she hadn't needed
to pack for Madeira.

The little windowless dressing room was no larger
than a cell, and yet a perfect contrast to her room at
Cornwall Gardens: comfortable and human. It was
lined like a jewel box in striped ivory silk with prints
of eighteenth-century ladies in flower-entwined swings.
The scent of face powder lingered in the air. But when
Karen looked into Mrs. Hoaresham's room, her great
canopied bed was already made. It was early yet, but
the old lady was already up and about her business.

Karen dressed in the only outfit she had and started
down the stairs. There was a hint of morning sunshine
from the window on the landing. She found Mrs.
Hoaresham at work in the kitchen, wearing an official-
looking cook's apron that reached to her shoes. She
was stirring batter in a brown bowl.

"What a treat to have the kitchen to myself and
someone to cook for," she said as a morning greeting.
"I send Cook away when the rest of the family's
gone." She whipped an extra puff of air into the bowl
of batter. "Spring comes early down here in Devon.
You'll find that young man of yours outdoors, com-
muning with nature."

Karen looked for him on the terrace, but she had it to herself. She sat down on the low stone retaining wall and gazed out across the sea. It was a beautiful gray-green with a mysterious island like a low table on the horizon. She watched the gulls turning in the sparkling air and thought suddenly of Lake Geneva. What a different scene. The little Wisconsin lake you could see across, where she and Jay had belly-flopped and dog-paddled and experimented with underwater goggles.

Had he said in his eleventh summer, "Someday when we're grown up, I'll marry you"? No, he hadn't said anything like that. The thought of it would have sent him scurrying. And yet it was the kind of thing girls liked to think small boys had said to them. What a pair of sheltered little innocents they'd been. Would she ever be able to remember that summer after this? And later, when she had time to think, would she be sorry that who she was would keep her from seeing him again?

She spotted Jay then. He was sitting on a little shelf of rock against the hillside, halfway down to the beach. He was facing away toward the crescent of sand. The wind caught his hair, blowing it to one side.

There was surely time for a walk before breakfast. She slipped over the stone wall and zigzagged down the hill to Jay. They strolled off then, hand-in-hand. A path materialized out of the undergrowth and wandered away from the sea, down toward the Saunton Sands Golf Club. The house was in the high distance behind them before either spoke.

"I could get to like this running-away bit," Jay said.

"It's only fun if no one's after you. I may have to make a lifetime career of it."

"It looks like you and I are going to have a big job just living our own lives." He told her then of his parents' plans for him. He'd been needing to talk about it all—Harvard, and then, inevitably, one of the family businesses. And a lifetime of Libertyville.

"It could be worse," Karen said.

"It's not what I want. Because it wouldn't be anything I'd done myself. I couldn't even pretend it was."

"What do you want?"

"That's funny. You're the first person who's ever bothered to ask. I've just started wondering myself. My folks sent me over here to Eton because it was a big prestige thing for them. I didn't realize it at the time, but it was something they were doing for themselves. And they'll keep right on doing it. Harvard, if I let them, and then—"

"And then the right Libertyville girl from the right Libertyville family."

"Yes," Jay said. "Even that."

"But you still haven't said what you want."

"I don't know. Maybe I want to drive a cab. Or do some construction work. Or swab decks on a tramp steamer. Sound crazy?"

"Not especially. You're looking for freedom. I'm trying to find a family that doesn't exist. Maybe we're both just trying to find ourselves."

"We've found each other. Maybe that's enough."

"No," Karen said. "It isn't."

The path led directly up to the low porch of the golf clubhouse. They turned then to start back. Karen was suddenly anxious again to make plans for getting home, any way she could.

Neither one of them noticed the man who was standing inside the clubhouse, watching. He was the grounds keeper for the club. An unimportant man, even to the organization he did an occasional job for. But he'd been alerted along with many others. The organization was very thorough, computerized, in fact. He had a hunch this was the girl they wanted back. They'd mentioned a boy too. And this was the sort of deserted, off-season place they might run to.

Perfect for them, except there is no perfect hiding place, especially on an island. He couldn't be sure, of course, until he'd had a look round for the car. But he always played his hunches. Time enough later to look for the car and check the license plates. He turned back to the office where the telephone was.

"The secret is in the sauce," Mrs. Hoarseham said, sinking her fork into the paper-thin pancakes that seemed to float above their plates. "I add a quarter cup of apricot brandy to the melted butter for a sauce. They could hardly fail to be superb! Of course it's scarcely a suitable English breakfast, but then to-morrow I shall be in France where food is accorded the respect due it.

"Which brings to mind the question at hand. Before I leave, your problems must be thoroughly sorted out." Mrs. Hoaresham dabbed at a glistening dot of butter in the corner of her mouth. "For you will certainly not be staying on here in my absence.

"Now first you, Jay. Tomorrow you will return to Eton."

"But—"

"It's all arranged."

"But, Mrs. Hoaresham, I'm not going to leave Karen until—did you say it's all *arranged?*" Jay's classic doubletake made Karen's lips twitch. He had the strong, shaved jaw of a man and the shocked look of a little boy. She had to concentrate to keep the smile down.

"It is," Mrs. Hoaresham went on calmly. "Your truancy has nearly run its course. I have rung up your house master to explain that you are in my charge. I must say he was quite civil about it. Apparently your fine record has purchased you some latitude. But there are limits. Naturally, you cannot stay away indefinitely. A fine example that would be to my grandson, who needs all the inspiration he can get."

Jay fumed in flabbergasted silence. But Karen said suddenly, "And I'll go to France with you, Mrs. Hoaresham. You're going by sea and then on to Paris, aren't you?"

"Of course. I never fly. And I always break my journey at Paris."

"Well, then I'll cross the Channel with you and try to get a plane home from Paris. Nobody will be looking for me at the Paris airport."

Mrs. Hoaresham was nodding with interest, but Jay said, "No, Karen, it won't work. The British police will be watching for you at the Channel ports. You have to clear customs there too. By now they might even have distributed a picture of you."

"One moment!" Mrs. Hoaresham said. "There is a way, practically foolproof. If Karen and I cross to Boulogne, she can travel without showing her passport on a day's excursion ticket. People go over for the day in droves from Folkestone. Of course, if we are questioned as we continue our journey to Paris, it could be awkward." Mes. Hoaresham was deep in thought for a moment.

"But I can deal with the French. I never speak their language. I shall pass you off as my personal maid, a silly goose who left her passport behind by mistake. Those French officials will be no match for me."

Karen and Jay were in silent agreement on that point.

12

Mrs. Hoaresham's preparations were elaborate. It took her most of the day to pack for Monte Carlo. Her spacious room was an obstacle course of folded linen, yawning suitcases, and even a battered wardrobe trunk emblazoned with dozens of faded labels. They all read *Hotel des Arts, Monaco,* and the oldest of them were far older than Karen.

She was pressed into service, while Jay prowled the house aimlessly. But by mid-afternoon he was put to work, too, forcing the suitcases shut and trundling them downstairs. He was tangled in the straps that bound the trunk when Mrs. Hoaresham turned to Karen with a lively look.

"And now," she said, " we come to the problem of a suitable disguise."

Karen and Jay glanced at each other.

"Well, you can hardly travel incognito looking like yourself, can you?"

"Won't this do?" Karen said gazing down at her good, serviceable tweed suit. "Wouldn't it pass as English?"

"English?" the old lady said in astonishment. "English? Certainly not! There's nothing English about it. It's as American as . . . as pumpkin pie, whatever that is. And it's rather too smart for a lady's maid in any case."

Mrs. Hoaresham bustled to one of her wardrobe cupboards. "I'm perhaps a size larger than you, or at least I was some years ago, which is all to the good. And I never throw anything out."

Jay cast his eyes toward the ceiling. Mrs. Hoaresham swept back. A dress, a coat, even a hat were piled over her arm. "Off you go," she said, waving Karen to the dressing room. "We'll have a sort of costume rehearsal." Mrs. Hoaresham was nearly bouncing with excitement.

Karen vanished, and Jay tried to concentrate on the problem of the trunk. Minutes passed. Suddenly she reappeared in the dressing-room door, looking mortified. The shapeless felt hat was a ghastly shade of mustard yellow and was pierced by a permanent-looking hatpin. Her hair hung limply down from under it. A calflength gray cloth coat seemed to envelop her without touching her body. The dress under it was a khaki-green crepe with a lace collar and hideous buttons that glittered with red glass. Karen's true shape seemed to have melted away, along with the rest of her identity.

"Good grief!" Jay said.

"Perfect," said Mrs. Hoaresham.

It was almost evening when Karen, dressed again in her own tweeds, found Jay deep in a chair in the lounge. By the fading light he was concentrating on a thick volume from the Hoaresham-D'ark library. The sun beyond the French windows was sinking into the sea.

She stood in the doorway, looking at his profile, thinking how far she would be from this moment tomorrow if all went well. He looked up then, and smiled.

"What are you reading?"

"Shakespeare. *Antony and Cleopatra.* I'm supposed

to be reading it with my tutor. Since Mrs. Hoaresham is sending me back, I thought I might as well be prepared."

"Read me something from it."

> *"The bright day is done,*
> *And we are for the dark*

A nice, suitable touch for the time of day, wouldn't you say?"

He put out his hand to her, and she walked over to take it. But Mrs. Hoaresham's voice in the distance broke the mood. She was quite ready for Jay to bring her wardrobe trunk downstairs. He stood up, and his lips brushed her forehead. He touched her hair gently, then loped off with a shrug of resignation and a wink.

Karen curled up in the warm hollow his body had made in the chair. She could nearly see past the complexities of getting home now. They were almost like details. It was time to prepare herself for what she would find when she got there. When she was with Dad. If he was alive.

A shadow from the long window fell across her knees. Too sudden for sunset. A form filled the French door. Karen jerked upright. Her eyes had almost drooped shut, and she'd barely noticed. She looked quickly past the wing of the chair. Not two feet from her she saw the man standing just outside, his face almost pressed against the pane. She stared at him, not knowing him in the first second, not believing in the second. It was Albert.

His hand was turning on the handle of the door. For the first time in her life, Karen was afraid she was going to faint. She started out of her chair, but every move was in slow motion. Only her mind leaped. Was the door unlocked? It wasn't the one they'd been going in and out of. Did it open inward or out? In, she was almost sure. Her eyes couldn't leave Albert's. Though his were in shadow, she could see the sagging lids, the dull look. He's feebleminded, she thought wildly. He seemed fascinated by her, by the terror in her face perhaps. His hand turned and turned on the handle, but he never took his empty eyes off her.

It's locked, she thought, but he could try the other door. It isn't. Her mind was full of the moment, too full to signal a scream. It went dead suddenly at the sound of broken glass. She looked down then. Albert's fist had plunged through the small pane beside the door handle. She could have reached out and touched him. His big fist worked in and closed around the knob on the inside.

She was on her feet then, acting without thinking. She grabbed the chair by its arms and jammed it back against the door. Albert's head jerked up. Had she hit his hand that was working the inside knob? Another small splash of broken glass as the rest of the pane fell on the floor.

Albert lunged against the door. The armchair skidded forward. Karen jumped back as the chair toppled in front of her. Only then did she remember to run.

She was halfway across the room before the scream built in her. She had run a half dozen paces, but it had only taken Albert a couple. His hand slammed around her mouth, cutting off the scream and jerking back her neck with a crack that spread across her shoulders in a hot pain.

He held her then for a moment. His huge hand closed on her mouth in a vise. He swung her around so quickly that she stumbled over her own feet. Then he caught up her arm and twisted it behind her. He could have broken both her neck and her arm in two quick movements. They stood there, facing the windows then, and she had time to know how he could kill her then if he wanted to.

I've got to think of something, but her mind was slipping away from her. She started to slump, but his hands only tightened, a sudden pressure to let her know how much more strength he had in reserve. He was marching her toward the door. The chair was in the way, but that wouldn't stop him. Beyond the terrace the sun dropped into the sea. Karen's mind followed it into the distance.

Albert's leg shot past her, and he kicked the chair aside, easily. He wrenched her arm and shoved her forward toward the open door. She was vaguely aware of the grit of glass under her shoe.

Then, a sudden blow sent her stumbling over the door sill. Something—it must have been Albert's head—had butted against her back with terrific force. The arm pinned behind her swung free, and his big hand slipped from her mouth. Too stunned to scream, she tripped and fell out on the paving stones of the terrace. Instinct made her roll to one side. And then she was up on her knees, feeling the prickly life flow back into her arm. Inside the living room she could hear a meaningless series of noises. A gasping grunt, the scrape of shoes in a kind of wild dance, the sound of something heavy falling. She looked away, to the low wall surrounding the terrace. Should she—

She was gulping down the cold sea air in deep breaths, crouched like an animal trying to save itself. Then she heard the sound of the other French door being thrown back. Someone was standing there, practically over her. With a dodging movement, she was on her feet and running across the terrace toward the wall. It was a short drop down to the sloping hillside. She didn't even need to ease herself over. She could take it at a run and leap down the other—

Jay caught her around the waist when she was almost airborne. He spun her around in his arms so she could see. So she would know she was safe.

He held her close to him for a moment, and then they walked back toward the house. The French doors were flung against the wall, pinning back the heavy curtains that fluttered and tried to escape in the evening breeze. The big room seemed as dark as a cave at first, but Karen saw Albert stretched on the floor in the patch of pale evening light.

"It wasn't a very gentlemanly fight," Jay said in a shaky voice. "I came up from behind and kicked him. Then when he let go of you, I got a couple of punches in before he knew what was happening."

"And I finished him off with a rather nice Wedgwood vase," Mrs. Hoaresham announced proudly. She stepped out of the shadows, looking as fragile and aristocratic as ever.

Albert's head lay face down in a welter of splintered glass mingled with pieces of black pottery.

"Is he—"

"No, I'm afraid not," Mrs. Hoaresham said. "He'll live. He is, I presume, Albert?"

The three of them stood there in the near darkness for a moment. No one needed to say it. They all knew they would have to get away at once.

Mrs. Hoaresham went in search of a length of rope to tie up Albert. Jay stood over him, watching for any sign of movement. Karen headed for the stairs to change to her disguise. With a little organization they could be out of the house and away in five minutes. Somehow, they'd been found. And Albert had been sent. But was he alone?

The big wardrobe trunk stood upside down at the foot of the stairs in the entrance hall. Jay must have sent it skidding down the steps when he'd heard noises in the living room. Karen was sidestepping it when someone knocked at the front door.

She froze. Was it her imagination? She held her

breath. Could Jay have heard it too? She didn't dare call out to him. There was a shuffle of feet outside on the front porch.

If she could move the trunk, she could slide it across the door. But that was pointless since the terrace doors at the back of the house were standing open. Anyone circling the house would come up behind Jay from the terrace side.

Karen reached out to the umbrella stand. Stuck down in among the umbrellas was a stout walking stick. She drew it out carefully and flattened herself against the wall. Then she unlatched the door with one hand and let it swing open.

Nothing. No one rushed in. In the last second she had a sudden recollection of Syd. Syd with his shoulder holster. She wheeled around to face whoever it was, swinging back with the walking stick.

The man on the porch shouted out something in a strangled voice and fell backwards off the step, sprawling in the gravel. It was dark out there, but she could see he was wearing some kind of a uniform. His cap rolled away in the direction of a van pulled up behind the car.

He lay there on his back, propped up by his elbows. His mouth hung open, and Karen could see the whites of his horrified eyes. He made no move, and only then did she begin to lower the walking stick. He must be unarmed. She could hear Jay and Mrs. Hoaresham rushing up behind her.

"Oh my heavens!" Mrs. Hoaresham said, pushing Karen to one side. "You've frightened Mr. Cobleigh! He's come for my trunk."

The words on the side of the van read *British Railways*. And old Mr. Cobleigh, who'd suffered a nasty shock, had to be helped up in stages. He was unsteady on his feet and needed to be coaxed into the house by

Mrs. Hoaresham, who hovered around him and
brushed gravel off his back.

When he saw the trunk, he regained a little control
and sent Jay out to the van for his two-wheeled cart.
He examined the load with a careful eye just as if he
hadn't been collecting that same trunk annually for
the past forty years. But he kept casting quick glances
toward Karen as if she might be expected to show
more signs of violence. She tried to stand between
him and the lounge in case he could catch sight of
Albert, unconscious and trussed up on the floor. She
would have expanded to fill the whole double doorway if she could. But Mr. Cobleigh seemed more interested in her than her background.

"My dear, you didn't actually *assault* him, did you?"
Mrs. Hoaresham murmured in passing.

Finally, with Jay's help, Mr. Cobleigh was easing
the trunk off the front porch step. Karen was ready
again to think of flight, but Mrs. Hoaresham stood at
the front door, waiting calmly for the trunk to be
loaded onto the van.

"Mr. Cobleigh, will you be good enough to come
back to the house for a moment, if you please!" she
called out into the night air. The hillside could be
alive with an army of homicidal maniacs, Karen
thought, and Mrs. Hoaresham would proceed calmly
at her own pace. Karen looked back again toward Albert and stationed herself squarely in the doorway to
the living room.

But when Mr. Cobleigh appeared again on the
porch, cap in hand and rather wary, Mrs. Hoaresham
drew him inside. Waving Karen away, she led the old
man into the living room, straight up to the spot
where Albert's enormous feet lay tightly bound together. "As you will see, Mr. Cobleigh, we have been
disturbed by an intruder."

Karen and Jay exchanged another of their quick glances, but both looked back to Mr. Cobleigh, who was having his second shock of the evening. He was far from recovered before Mrs. Hoaresham continued in a flowing, everyday voice. "You may imagine our horror at surprising this housebreaker in our midst. Which will, of course, explain the young lady's reaction when you appeared at the front door only moments later.

"Now, Mr. Cobleigh, I wonder if we might impose upon your good nature in asking you a *great* favor." Mr. Cobleigh could hardly take his dazed eyes off Albert. "My young friends and I are leaving for the continent this evening, and of course we *cannot* be delayed by this distressing occurrence. And so here is how you will be able to help us."

Mrs. Hoaresham's voice became low and confidential as she explained to Mr. Cobleigh exactly what she wanted him to do. His eyes grew even rounder, but there was something about her powers of persuasion that he couldn't resist. Before she was finished, he was nodding unconsciously in rhythm to every word she spoke.

The plan she outlined was to involve Mr. Cobleigh to the limits of his usefulness. And he was far too interested in his part to ask any question. Mrs. Hoaresham explained that the unknown intruder had boldly drawn up in the car parked outside, the car Karen and Jay had driven down from London. "I expect you will find the keys still in it," she said in a ringing voice that sent Jay rummaging through his pockets. He slipped away then, behind Mr. Cobleigh, to replace the keys in the car.

Mrs. Hoaresham explained that in order to prevent further delays, it would be wiser to place the intruder in his car and drive it down the headland road to the next turn-off. Mr. Cobleigh and Jay would be able to carry the unconscious body to the car and to remove the car to this safe distance.

Then, when Mrs. Hoaresham and her young friends had departed, Mr. Cobleigh was to notify the local police that he had noticed a suspicious car parked at the roadside when he passed in his van. "And," she concluded, "I should consider it a *great* favor if you did not mention anything about the man's having entered this house. After all, I shouldn't like being troubled on my holiday."

Mr. Cobleigh was putty in her hands. "How *much* we appreciate your help," Mrs. Hoaresham said, clinching the deal.

When Albert came to, he found himself bound hand and foot in a strange car on a strange road, not far from the sea. His dull head was cracking with pain. Various other parts of his big body were either cramped or sore or both. It would have taken a quick thinker to figure out what he was doing there or to remember what his instructions had been, exactly what Syd and Blanche had sent him into the house to do. But Albert was a very slow thinker.

He couldn't remember when he'd left the Suttons in their car down by the golf club. He couldn't remember creeping up the path from the golf course to the big house on the hill. And though the knuckles on one hand were skinned and raw, he couldn't remember sticking his fist through the glass panel. He could only concentrate on his pain and the glare of light pouring through the windshield and into his eyes. The glare from Syd's flashlight.

But the voice was Blanche's hissing out from the darkness beyond. "The great oaf! *The great stupid oaf!* Leave him and let the police find him. He's worse than useless!"

"Now, Blanche, it wouldn't do—" Syd's whine withered even before Blanche snapped back at him.

"Do what you like with him. At least get the car well away from here. Take it back to London. You're both worthless. They're leaving, and I'll follow them in our car. I'll get the girl back myself. You know what'll happen to us if she gets away. You do know, don't you, Syd?"

13

The little tea shop called The Cameo wasn't really
open for business. It was tucked back along a quiet
side street above the Folkestone harbor, twenty fog-
bound miles from the shore of France. The Cameo
generally did no serving earlier than eight in the morning.

But well before that, three people were having
breakfast in the most private corner of the room. The
sleepy, sullen waitress tried to turn them away. But
the elderly lady in the silk turban and the fox furs
insisted. She'd arrived in her large Rolls Royce with a
blond young man who might either be her grandson
or her chauffeur. And the dowdy young woman with
her was obviously her maid.

Mrs. Hoaresham looked down into her basin of clot-
ted gray porridge. "Ah," she said, "my last English
breakfast for a while. Yours too, of course," she nodded toward Karen. "But as for you, Jay, tomorrow you
will be back savoring the gastronomic delights of
Wykeham House." Mr. Hoaresham smoothed the napkin in her lap with precise fingers. She was always very
bright at breakfast, even after a sleepless night.

"Yes, I did think," she said, lowering her voice, "that
it was rather acute of me to think of dumping Albert
in the car you'd, uh, confiscated. Of course, we could
have driven down here in it, but it might have been

identified. It was much more satisfactory to dispose of two objects of embarrassment at once—Albert *and* the car. And of course, my old Rolls is so much more comfortable. You can have it garaged here for me, Jay, and I shall pick it up on my return from Monte Carlo.

"I do wonder if they managed to find poor Albert," she said, her eyes flashing with wicked mirth. "The local Devon authorities are not what one might call quick off the mark."

"What if Albert talks?" Jay asked. "The police might try to contact you before you leave the country, even if they don't know about Karen."

"I think it very unlikely," she replied. "I always cross the Channel from Dover to Calais. Everybody knows that. If they wanted to reach me, they'd send word there. But here we are at Folkestone, where of course we are making only a brief junket to the French coast because," he eyes flashed again at Karen "one of us doesn't have a proper British passport."

The waitress brought plates of eggs and sausages as a reward for their getting through the porridge. They ate in silence then. It had been a long night, with Jay at the wheel, driving halfway across southern England. Karen had sat in the back with Mrs. Hoaresham, bundled in a heavy lap robe.

She'd watched the road ahead and Jay's hands on the oversized steering wheel. And she'd kept glancing behind them out of the narrow rear window. Headlights had seemed to follow them through most of the night. But they had traveled busy roads, and Karen tried to relax, even though she couldn't sleep.

Mrs. Hoaresham arranged her furs and stood up. "We won't appear at the boat for a few minutes more, I think. It will be as well to arrive at the last moment. I shall go out to the car while you young people say your good-byes." She sailed out of the tea shop.

"She thinks of everything," Jay said as the door closed behind her. But Mrs. Hoaresham seemed to have taken all the conversation with her. After a pause that went on too long, Jay said, "Where will I find you when I come back home?"

"I don't know," Karen said. She wanted a quick good-bye. And yet she wanted these minutes to last. "I don't know where I'll be or . . . anything."

"After you've seen your father, you'll go back to school, won't you?"

"I haven't thought it out that far. No, that's not true. Even when I've been thinking about Dad, I've been wondering what it would be like back at school. I was never sure before whether people knew or not. But now there's no question about that. I don't quite know yet how I'll face them. You know I might contaminate the reputations of all those girls from good families. The Isobel Kelvin Academy doesn't cater to the criminal element."

"Don't talk like that."

"It's just everything's going to be so different now. All those things that seemed so sure and important to that little boarding-school girl I used to be are all meaningless now. I don't think I'll fit in with all those prep-school types anymore. They haven't found out yet that they're going to have to grow up."

Karen got up then and wrapped the threadbare gray coat around her ghastly green dress. With both hands she settled the shapeless hat down farther over her ears. "Hey, don't look so depressed," she said, smiling down at Jay. "The next time we meet, I'll have a whole new wardrobe."

The Rolls Royce crept silently up to the pier and stopped under a sign that announced the ferry for Boulogne-Sur-Mer. A young man got out and removed two ancient leather suitcases from the trunk. He opened the rear door, from which an elderly lady in a turban and furs alighted. Behind her a rather mousy girl carrying a small overnight bag followed. A porter darted out to collect the luggage as the boat horn sounded a final warning.

There was no one left behind to notice that the tall, blond young man kissed the mousy girl good-bye.

The Rolls Royce edged away then, leaving the scene deserted. Fog boiling in from the channel nearly enveloped the gangplank that still connected boat and dock.

Across the cobblestone street a bell jangled as a woman in a raincoat plunged out of the door of a chemist shop. She raced across the empty street, jamming a bottle of seasick pills into her handbag as she ran. She hated boats, but she had to catch this one. It was her last chance. Everything depended on her. Everyone else was useless. She made it up the gangplank in the last seconds.

There was a scraping sound as the boat slipped past the pier, heading into a thick brew of fog and sea. Only a handful of "day trippers" were braving the elements for a few hours of France. A party of four men in golf caps settled at a card table in the far corner of the main salon. A schoolteacher lined up a class of damp, uniformed children to drill them at the last minute on a few useful French verbs. Mrs. Hoaresham and Karen sat at a table by a porthole bolted shut against the salt spray that pounded at it like rain.

"It is just as well, I find, to order coffee and biscuits if a crossing promises to be rough," Mrs. Hoaresham announced. "They keep the stomach occupied."

Karen was glad to leave England behind, but she felt the first queasy reaction to the open channel as one end of the long salon room rose, hesitated, and fell.

In a running crouch a waiter approached their table

balancing a tray of china in one hand and a large pitcher in the other. He poured a puddle of water directly onto the tablecloth, dampening it enough to keep the cups and saucers in place. Then he slopped a half measure of coffee into each cup. Mrs. Hoaresham eyed this performance with approval.

Karen could get the cup halfway to her mouth before the ship rolled in some new direction. "I nearly poured that mouthful down my ear," she said. Her strange, shapeless maid's hat rode on her head at an alarming angle.

"You'll soon have the knack of it," said Mrs. Hoaresham, looking as if she could balance a whole tray of crockery on her knee if she felt like it. "From the corner of my eye," she went on in the same tone, "I note that a uniformed personage is ciriculating amongst the passengers to examine their tickets. This would, I should imagine, be a wise time for you to slip away and see to our luggage, Karen. No point in his getting a good look at you if it can be avoided. I noticed our bags were heaped in a great jumble near the gangplank entrance."

Karen rose, dropped a fake maid's curtsey to which Mrs. Hoaresham nodded briefly. "Take this pound note and persuade a deck hand to find an empty compartment for the cases. I'm sure the compartments are quite unoccupied except for the odd seasick passenger. Leave your ticket with me."

Karen staggered off across the room, trudging uphill part of the way, skidding down the rest. She aimed at the double doorway at the end of the room and sprinted through it. The ship's officer continued his round. When he came to Mrs. Hoaresham, she dealt with him so firmly that he only glanced at the two round-trip tickets lying on the damp table before her.

He was no sooner gone than a woman approached

her from across the slanting salon. She wore a rain-coat and a very English canvas hat pulled low on her brow. Clutching a handbag, she bobbed her head to-ward the old lady in a little birdlike gesture.

"I'm terribly sorry to disturb you—isn't it a wretched crossing? I feel quite ill—but it's about the young woman traveling with you—"

"My maid?" Mrs. Hoaresham arched her eyebrows.

"Well, yes, I suppose so. She's had rather a nasty fall, I'm afraid. They've taken her to a stateroom, and she's asking for you."

Mrs. Hoaresham started from her chair. An empty coffee cup rolled out of its saucer and smashed on the floor. She waved the woman ahead of her, and they hurried off across the salon, making for the double doors.

They crossed a drafty area piled high with hand luggage, parcels, and bicycles. Two long hallways lined with the closed doors of empty cabins led for-ward. The woman in the raincoat darted down the hall on the starboard side. Mrs. Hoaresham managed to keep almost abreast of her. The ship pitched and rolled, and the two women staggered from one wall to the other. Near the darkened end of the hall, the woman in the raincoat opened a door partway and said into the emptiness beyond, "May we come in?" She turned quickly then and stepped aside allowing Mrs. Hoaresham to enter.

The door opened on a deserted cabin, furnished only with a bunk bed. Mrs. Hoaresham started to turn back. But the woman placed her hand against the old lady's back and pushed her roughly into the room. The door closed behind them.

Karen emerged from the hallway on the port side with a steward. He'd been almost-but-not-quite too polite to accept the pound note for leaving her luggage in an empty compartment. Somewhat puzzled by the contrast between her face and her clothes, he held the door open for her as she returned to the salon.

She saw at once that Mrs. Hoaresham had left their table. Then she noticed the shattered cup on the floor. She sat down, bracing herself against the roll of the ship and the uneasy feeling that something had gone wrong. The minutes passed, and Mrs. Hoaresham didn't return. She glanced at her watch. The ship should be in mid-channel by now, halfway to France unless it was only inching along through the weather and high seas.

She thought of asking the man in the uniform—the deck officer—if he'd noticed where Mrs. Hoaresham went. Almost catching his eye, she thought better of it. Instead, she turned away and stared at the streaming porthole.

It was stifling the room. The school children across the salon were growing strangely quiet and their faces were turning varying shades of green. Karen was finding it harder to swallow. The table top had a tendency to loom up at her suddenly. She stood then and made her way across to the double doors.

It was cooler out among the parcels and bicycles. The steward who had helped her with the luggage swept by carrying a pile of basins and towels into the salon. Both corridors leading toward the bow of the ship were dark and deserted. She turned and pushed through a heavy door out onto the open deck.

There was the sound of gulls screaming between the steady blasts of the fog horn. Karen looked up the deck, not really expecting to find Mrs. Hoaresham at the mercy of the elements. But there was a woman standing beside the rail, almost lost in the wispy mist. Karen walked toward her.

They were near enough to touch when the woman

turned abruptly and said, "Hello, Karen." It was Blanche.

It couldn't be, but it was. Karen's mind whirled. She could feel the heaving deck under her feet. Too wet and hazardous to run even if she hadn't been rooted to the spot. Blanche's hands worked on the clasp of her purse. "You've led me a merry chase, my dear," she said. "It stops here."

Her voice was low and steely, no longer birdlike. "I don't know what that absurd costume you're wearing is meant to represent—a maid's disguise according to the old woman—but I assure you the time for play-acting is over for both of us."

"What do you want from me?" Karen said, not yet absorbing the mention of Mrs. Hoaresham.

"I? Nothing at all. What I want doesn't matter. I have been instructed to bring you back. You are to be held, this time as a prisoner. Your father, as you know perfectly well, has refused to come to terms with powers infinitely more important than himself. He will come to terms and he will hand over his authority in New York if it means seeing you again. Assuming he's still alive."

"And if he's not?" Karen heard herself saying.

"In that event, you'll be disposed of. And while we're on the subject, it would be better for me to kill you at this moment and throw you overboard than to return without you. I trust that's quite clear?" Blanche opened the clasp of her bag. "There's a revolver in here. I wouldn't hesitate to use it." Karen stared at the handbag Blanche's hand was thrust into. She felt strangely detached. She even thought of Syd's shoulder holster and of how much more likely a killer Blanche was.

Blanche's hand, buried in the bag, dislodged a small vial of white pills that threatened to fall out of the purse. She fumbled to retrieve them before they spilled onto the deck. But she stepped back and her hand seemed to close on an unseen object within the purse at the same moment.

"Now here's precisely what we're going to—"

"Where is Mrs. Hoaresham?"

"The doddery old party in the fox furs? I knew you'd come looking for her, and I meant you to find me first. She'll serve as part of the plan. Shut up and listen."

The first shock hadn't faded from Karen's mind. But she noticed odd bits of detail. Blanche's voice was even and cutting. But her color was bad. Her cheeks, washed clean of powder by the sea spray, were an ugly shade of gray-yellow.

". . . old fool is trussed up like a turkey in an empty stateroom where she will stay for the . . ."

Karen stared at Blanche, almost relieved at being able to hate her at last.

By balancing her handbag on her knee, Blanche captured the pill bottle and was trying to unscrew the cap with two fingers. Her other hand stayed in the bag, and her eyes never left Karen's. She's sick, Karen thought. She's seasick.

". . . go quietly back to the stateroom where I will certainly kill the old woman if you don't do precisely as you're told. The three of us will stay on the boat and return to England on it. We'll say the weather's too bad for going ashore at Boulogne. And once we're back, I'll be taking you to a place where you'll be well looked after."

"And what happens to Mrs. Hoaresham?"

"She can go free at Folkestone. Who'd believe the rantings of an old fool? And besides, you and I will be well away before she can do anything."

She'll kill her, Karen thought. She'll kill Mr. Hoaresham. She'll have to. Leave her in the stateroom, dead.

It was as clear to Karen as if it had already happened. Maybe it has, she thought.

Blanche had finally coaxed two pills from the bottle and was silent as she tried to swallow them without water. "Water, water everywhere, nor any drop to drink." Karen's mind quoted insanely. Along the empty deck she saw the shore of France looming up. The horn blasted deafeningly. Blanche swallowed and spun Karen around. The two of them began walking back toward the door that led to the ship.

Karen stopped. "There's just one thing," she said over her shoulder.

"Be quick."

"The picture. The one on the piano. It wasn't of my . . . it wasn't of Eleanor."

"Of course not, you little idiot. How could it be? I bought it myself in a junk shop."

"Thank God."

"What?"

"Thank God it wasn't a picture of you."

They walked on. Karen's ideas tried to race ahead of her. She knew they'd surely have to pass some of the crew or the passengers. She believed Blanche would kill her if she couldn't take her back alive, but only if she could get away herself. And only Blanche knew where she'd left Mrs. Hoaresham "trussed up like a turkey." Why don't I let her take me back, Karen thought—briefly—if it means Mrs. Hoaresham will be safe? But it wouldn't mean that. And what about Dad?

There was something else, though. Something nibbling at the edge of Karen's mind. The passage between the salon and the corridors of the staterooms was filling with travelers anxioius to tread solid ground. The stewards were lined up smartly, wearing their going-ashore caps. The deck officer was untangling bicycles and golf bags for the passengers.

Karen hesitated in the doorway long enough to feel Blanche thump her hard in the small of the back. It was Blanche's fist, Karen thought, not the muzzle of the gun. Fifteen or twenty paces across to the nearer corridor. Mrs. Hoaresham must be down there, she thought, unless she was put in the same corridor where our luggage is. Now or never, she said to herself. Probably never.

Then it dawned on her. It was only a theory, probably a wild one. But she needed to believe in it. *She hadn't seen the gun in Blanche's purse.* Not quite. Blanche wanted her to think it was there. But it wasn't. Blanche couldn't risk it. She was playing a role again, as she had at Cornwall Gardens, and staying on the safe side in case she was discovered. It was Blanche's way.

But the trouble with theories . . .

The deck officer looked up from his last-minute duties, surprised and displeased to see two passengers coming in from the deck where they shouldn't have been in this weather. He noticed the girl in the old clothes first, though he couldn't remember checking her ticket. He started over to her, vaguely aware of how closely behind her the other woman was walking.

Karen fixed her eyes on him, trying to draw him closer, faster. If her theory was right, if Blanche didn't have a gun, what could she say? They'd think she was crazy, and somehow Blanche would make good use of that.

Blanche had seen the officer heading their way. She nudged Karen. An ominous reminder.

"Officer. Please," Karen's voice rang out in the noisy room of strangers. She felt something thrust sharply into her back. But it felt more like the clasp of a handbag than the barrel of a gun. She almost smiled in relief or triumph. But it was too early for either.

"Yes, Miss?" he said, smiling genially and blocking their way.

"This woman," Karen sidestepped Blanche quickly. "This woman asked me to carry a bottle of pills ashore for her. She says they're seasick pills but that can't be true, can it? They must be something else, mustn't they? Something illegal?"

Blanche gasped. But she was no more stunned than Karen was herself. Where had the idea come from? The gun, that possibly wasn't there, and the pills that were. And her little speech, so innocent, with just a touch of an English accent.

"You bloody little bitch!" Blanche barked out, sealing her fate. Every head in the room turned.

"Here now. None of that," the officer reached out to Blanche, who quivered with rage. Karen took a step away. Then two steps. "If you wouldn't mind just showing me the pills."

"They *are* seasick pills. That girl's mad. I said no such thing to her. I don't even know who she is!" Blanche was screaming now.

"What's the matter with that lady?" one of the children asked his teacher. The passengers moved forward, ringing the officer and Blanche. She jerked open the handbag. And pulled out the bottle of pills. There was no gun.

"You see? An ordinary bottle of patent medicine. A perfectly respectable label!" Her words were nearly swallowed by the shrillness of her voice. Her eyes shifted from side to side, wildly. "Where is that girl? Where did she go? I'll—"

"Here now," the officer said, catching her by the arms. "We'll have to have a look at the pills. Have them analyzed."

"Well, do it then!" Blanche shrieked.

"We'll have to send them ashore to a lab. And I'm

afraid we'll have to hold you until we have the re-
sults."

"You can't hold me. It's against the law."

Then Blanche lost her head completely, whirled
and darted for the open deck. The stewards broke
rank and jammed through the door after her. And the
curious passengers surged after them.

Karen receded into the darkness of the starboard
corridor, almost invisible in the midst of the double
row of cabin doors. Even during Blanche's shrieks and
the low rumble of the officer's voice, Karen had
melted from the scene. She was trying each door as
she came to it. They all seemed unlocked and empty.
She knew there'd only be minutes before she'd be
drawn back into the scene she'd created. She wasn't
even aware of the wave of passengers who flocked out
onto the deck behind Blanche.

The door of the inside cabin at the end was locked.
The noises behind her were suddenly gone. "Mrs.
Hoaresham, are you in there? Can you hear me?" Her
hand twisted on the little knob.

Silence. Karen turned to try the other corridor, hoping there'd be time. But she heard a sound inside
then. The sound of a heavy object falling on the cabin
floor. Someone was in there. But the sound was
frightening, inhuman.

She pressed her shoulder against the door. It was
flimsy, and it gave, but not enough. She stood back
and hoisted up her flowing gray coat with both
hands. Then she gave the door an almighty kick with
the flat of her foot.

Then two more, mightier than the first. The door
burst back, banging the wall. Inside, it was as dark as
a pocket. Karen slid her hand over the wall to find the
switch.

In the sudden light the rear wall of the windowless

cabin loomed at her. There was only room for a bunk. But there on the narrow strip of floor lay Mrs. Hoaresham, unmoving.

She was lying face down. Karen noticed her hands first, tiny and white and twisted behind her back. Then the strips of cloth that bound her wrists. And the knot of cloth at the back of her head.

"Oh no," Karen whispered, "don't be dead." She fell on her knees and tried to turn the old lady over. She moved like an elongated doll, and Karen saw that her ankles were bound with strips of the same cloth. Her furs were bunched around her neck. Two fox heads with mean, beady eyes covered Mrs. Hoaresham's face. Her silk turban lay in the corner, with the Paris label hanging down by a thread.

Karen pulled the foxes away from her face with almost uncontrollable fingers, to find the cloth bound round her mouth. Mrs. Hoaresham's lips moved even before Karen could pull the gag away. "Those beastly furs very nearly strangled me. Such old friends too!"

Karen moaned with relief, and her eyes suddenly stung. "Now if you could just unbind my hands and feet," the victim was saying in her normal tone of command, "I can begin to restore my circulation. I had to throw myself on the floor to attract your attention."

Without even staggering, Karen managed to lift her up on the bunk to begin work on the hard knots. "That wretched woman *is* resourceful," Mrs. Hoaresham remarked, wincing a little as Karen jerked the knots loose. "She hadn't any rope about her, but she was quick enough to tear the bunk cover into strips— *while*, my dear, she sat on me."

"Oh, Mrs.—"

"Never mind, I'm quite all right. And I know who the wretched creature is, of course. Your false cousin,

Blanche. Quite a low type. She very nearly unnerved me. But never mind about that. What have you managed to accomplish?"

Karen outlined the situation briefly, while she massaged Mrs. Hoareshams's ankles.

"Accused her of being a smuggler of narcotics? A very nice touch indeed! It's probably the only crime she hasn't committed recently!"

The boat was suddenly calm, rocking gently at the pier after all its pitching and tossing in the open channel.

"And now," Karen said, "we have a choice. We can lie low in here and hope they think we've gone ashore. Or we can try to get away without being seen. I'm not up to risking another confrontation with Blanche. Especially if they try to hold me while they figure out what the pills are. And I don't think I want to be there when they find out they really are for seasickness."

"No, indeed," Mrs. Hoaresham said, swinging her feet onto the floor and exercising her ankles experimentally. "You've kept from being detained by the authorities so far. We must manage to leap this final hurdle."

"If it is the final one," Karen said.

"One step at a time," Mrs. Hoaresham said thoughtfully. "I have it! You must go ashore as yourself, not as a maid!"

Karen glanced down at the costume that had become a part of her. "Yes, that's it," she said. "I'll go for my case and make a quick change—"

"Oh no you won't," Mrs. Hoaresham said as she tottered to her feet. "No one must see you until you are transformed into your former self. Then no one could possibly make the connection—"

"Except Blanche," Karen said.

But Mrs. Hoaresham was ready for action again.

She staggered a bit, but she was herself again, arranging her choker of furs while Karen rescued her turban. "I think you had better sit in the dark until I return." She flipped out the light and made a dignified exit.

Sitting on the edge of the bunk in the blackness, Karen listened to Mrs. Hoaresham's high heels tapping down the corridor. Then her voice rose and echoed back, "Young man! I say, young man! Those appear to be my bags you are wheeling off. I need that smallest case before I go ashore. Yes, that one! No, I am aware that everyone else has disembarked. But I cannot be hurried!"

In the darkness, Karen smiled.

The last two passengers off the boat from Folkestone stepped onto French soil unnoticed. Even if the day had been sunny, the old lady might have passed as a duchess. And the lovely young girl beside her with the long brushed hair and the smart tweed suit might have been anybody but a maid. Behind them in a darkened stateroom lay a shapeless hat, a gray coat, and a ghastly green dress with red glass buttons.

They passed through an empty customs shed. No one challenged them even when the old lady waved a local taxi driver to her trunks. In a room not far away, the entire crew of border guards was preoccupied by a screaming hysterical Blanche. Blanche, who in the long run had not been a very useful member of her organization.

14

Rain blurred the windows of the Paris train, reminding Karen of the channel ferry's streaming portholes. While Mrs. Hoaresham dozed peacefully in the swaying seat across from her, Karen began at last to breathe.

Even Blanche was fading from her mind, receding into a dream. A dream of faces: Mrs. Plasket bending over her in the night; Albert's dull eyes staring at her through the windowed door; Jay, whose face she'd remember if she could. And her father as he'd looked on that long-ago day at the Plaza. Handsome, confident, in command of his secret world. Still three thousand miles away, she felt herself near to him at last, perhaps as near as she could ever be.

Mrs. Hoaresham stirred and spoke, possibly from a dream of her own, "If the conductor comes by again, I shall deal . . ."

Suddenly, Karen remembered the letters. Funny that they should come back to her now. The unmailed ones she used to write to Jay, a little-boy-far-away Jay replaced now by a real one. The letters she used to write on scraps of ruled school paper to push back the loneliness.

How hard she'd tried to call out then, hoping someone would hear—a boy who'd hardly existed for her then—and a father who could never dare to exist for her at all. She'd never be lonely like that again, and she knew it. She'd learned to be stronger than that.

At the station in Paris it was time for Karen and Mrs. Hoaresham to part. The strange little taxis were jockeying for position at the curb. Mrs. Hoaresham boomed commands in English at the porter who was piling her luggage into a cab. In a few minutes she'd be drawing up at the same Hotel de Castille in the rue Cambon where she always broke her journey to Monte Carlo. She was slipping back into her customary routine as smoothly as she had slipped out of it.

Is this the elderly lady who lay bound and gagged on the floor of a ship's stateroom a few hours ago? Karen's mind jumped from that image to concentrate on the last words she might ever hear from her.

"You've been quite wonderful, my dear."

"How can I thank you, Mrs. Hoaresham?"

"Thank me? What nonsense! Our exploits have made me feel quite forty years younger. You know, I believe that somehow in the space of a few hours you've grown up and I've grown young. One can but be grateful for such experiences. Of course, I shall breathe nothing of any of this to my friends. It is so tiresome to be disbelieved."

Then she was gone. And Karen was instructing a cab driver in her best third-year French to take her to Orly Airport.

When she bought her ticket there, she notified the Air France people that the New York police were looking for her. The message was conveyed without fuss or noticeable curiosity.

In less than half an hour, she was on a plane. The purser himself led her to a seat in the deserted first-class section, though she'd bought a tourist-class ticket. It had cost every dollar Blanche had never let her spend. She was offered champagne she didn't want and was discreetly guarded for six long hours.

Till the very moment the plainclothesmen moved toward her in the customs room at JFK. They flipped their badges open, their own kind of greeting, for they knew her from her picture as she walked off the plane. *Karen Beatty, 16, lured from her fashionable boarding school* in her tweed suit with her brown hair brushed smoothly over her shoulders.

In minutes she was led past the popping bulbs of the newspaper photographers, hurried out of the sound of the reporters' high-pitched questions:

"Miss Beatty, can you tell us about your abduction during your father's—"

"Miss Beatty, when did you first realize that—"

"Hey, Miss Beatty, Karen, give us a smile!"

"Miss Beatty, what are you going to say to your father when you—"

The door of the police car banged shut on the questions. But the last one lingered in Karen's mind. There was something about riding in a car full of polite policemen that made her feel half criminal and half victim. To her first questioning glance, they responded with no questions of their own. Time enough for that later. Yes, your father's alive. He's going to be all right. He's waiting to see you.

The skyline of Manhattan rose gray and glowing ahead. It was early evening, though for Karen it was midnight. Nearly a new day.

Her father's lawyers were at the hospital, as polite as the policemen. Knowing she'd be deaf to anything said to her, they led her to the door of her father's room. A nurse cracked the door and gave her a nod that was neither a welcome nor a warning.

Nothing stood between Karen and the white mound on the high hospital bed. It was strangely like being alone in the room. She walked nearer—across the last distance. The final question from the reporter came back to her. *What are you going to say to your father?*

But she knew the words wouldn't matter. Seeing that she was safe would be enough for him. It would have to be.

He'd always determined the distance between them and measured it in her innocence. And that had led them both too close to disaster. From now on Karen meant to determine the distance between them herself. And to measure it in truth.

When he sensed her standing beside the bed, he reached out his hand, and she took it, wordlessly.

Richard Peck

AWARD-WINNING MYSTERIES

LAUREL-LEAF BOOKS

by Joan Lowery Nixon

☐ **THE KIDNAPPING OF CHRISTINA LATTIMORE**
$1.75 (94520-8)
When her kidnappers claim that she was an accomplice to their crime, Christina and a young reporter set out to prove her innocence.

☐ **THE SEANCE**
$1.75 (97937-4)
It started as a game, with Lauren and five other girls gathered in a candlelit circle. But one-by-one, the participants were being murdered—and Lauren could be next.

Both books are winners of the Edgar Allan Poe Mystery Writers Award.

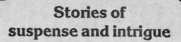